F
PIN

## DATE DUE

| JAN 21 '92 | | | |
|---|---|---|---|
| FEB 24 '90 | | | |
| | | | |
| | | | |
| | | | |
| | | | |
| | | | |
| | | | |
| | | | |
| | | | |
| | | | |
| | | | |
| | | | |
| | | | |
| | | | |

F

# The
# Disappearance
# of Sister Perfect

# The Disappearance of Sister Perfect

## JILL PINKWATER

E. P. Dutton    New York

*Library of Congress Cataloging in Publication Data*

Pinkwater, Jill.
    The disappearance of Sister Perfect.

    Summary: Sherelee Holmes, who claims to be
descended from Sherlock, investigates the peculiar
behavior of her older sister and ends up going
undercover into the compound of a dangerous
religious cult.
    [1. Cults—Fiction.   2. Sisters—Fiction.
3. Mystery and detective stories]   I. Title.
PZ7.P6336Di   1987   [Fic]   86-16676
ISBN 0-525-44278-2

Published in the United States by E. P. Dutton,
2 Park Avenue, New York, N.Y. 10016

Published simultaneously in Canada by
Fitzhenry & Whiteside Limited, Toronto

Editor: Ann Durell    Designer: Isabel Warren-Lynch

Printed in the U.S.A.   W   First Edition
10 9 8 7 6 5 4 3 2 1

for Daniel Pinkwater and Sherlock Holmes

# 1

My name is Sherelee Holmes. I am a detective. I am also the great-great-granddaughter of Sherlock Holmes, the greatest detective of all time. Probably you have heard of him.

Great-great-grandpa Sherlock was the first detective in our family. I have learned most of what I know about solving crimes from reading accounts of his adventures. All of Great-great-grandpa's cases were carefully recorded by his good friend and biographer, Dr. John H. Watson. I have a Watson, too. Joan H. Watson is my best friend. We have known each other our whole lives.

The fact that I am a Holmes and a detective means nothing to the kids at school. Rather than being impressed with my family tree or my abilities, they show no interest whatsoever. Even Joan Watson usually behaves just like my other classmates. Sometimes I have to bribe or threaten in order to capture Watson's attention when I want to discuss detecting theories.

Watson should be writing the account of my first big case. Every great detective should have an admiring friend and biographer who is able to record exploits, feats of mental brilliance and acts of bravery. It sounds like bragging when the detective is forced to write about herself. Joan Watson's worst school subject is English. She can't spell, punctuate or think enough thoughts to make a whole paragraph.

Joan H. Watson is not an ideal Watson for a detecting Holmes, but she's all I have at the moment. Besides, she is very loyal and usually trustworthy. Great detectives learn to adapt to circumstances beyond our control.

For example, my family has decided to deny we are related to Great-great-grandpa Sherlock. Dad calls me a Looney Tune and says things like, "No one can be related to a fictional character. Sherlock Holmes was a figment of Sir Arthur Conan Doyle's imagination." My mother, who has always been suspicious of my father's family, says, "Stop telling people you are descended from a fictional character—besides, Sherlock Holmes never got married."

Mother follows that statement up with a lot of muttering. If you bother to listen, you can hear her say things like, "Well, you know, Uncle Melvin was always a little bit fictional . . . and there was Aunt Mildred, who said she was fictional. I guess there's somebody fictional in most families. . . . Nevertheless, Sherelee, please stop saying your father's family has fictional people in it . . . it just doesn't seem right."

Of course he was real. I am his great-great-granddaughter, and I am real. You would think my family would be proud to accept the legacy. You would think they would encourage me as I developed my nimble mental powers. It's simply one more circumstance of life to which I have learned to adjust. I will carry on the Holmes tradition. Someday I will be as famous as Great-great-grandfather.

Which brings us to the point of this writing—my first important case. Great-great-grandpa Sherlock had an older brother, Mycroft. They didn't get along. Mycroft gave Sherlock trouble whenever he could. Mycroft was a genius, so the trouble he created was usually interesting and challenging.

I have a sister, Myra. She is not a genius, but she makes plenty of trouble anyway. Myra is the subject of this case.

# 2

I have never gotten along with my sister, Myra—she never gave me a chance. Myra was here first.

She was the first child, the first niece, the first grandchild, the first cousin and the first cute little baby to arrive in our huge family. For three years, her feet never touched ground at family gatherings. She went from lap to lap and from hug to hug. Myra loved it. She must have had a hundred toys by the time she was two. No adult dared show up empty-handed when Myra was to be visited. Not that Myra would have ever noticed. She had more toys than any ten kids could handle. Toy giving had become a family competition. If one set of grandparents bought Myra a teddy bear, the other set would show up next time with a stuffed elephant. The same went for the five sets of aunts and uncles. It was rumored that Uncle Jack and Aunt Phonecia once tried to apply for a toy loan when they were broke, but the bank turned them down.

You might say Myra was a little bit spoiled by all this attention. Myra, of course, figured she had been born into a sort of kid heaven. Then my cousins Joe, Susan, Ralph, Edgar and Amy were born. Then I came along. Myra must have been an inspiration because all of us kids arrived during a three-year period of time. Myra went into shock.

There were no more free laps. The present competition ground to a halt. With all the new babies around, Myra found herself on the edge of things. One day, entering a room filled with burping, gurgling, babbling, cute, cuddly babies and toddlers, Myra realized that not just for that moment or for the next year or until she grew up—but for always—she would be the oldest. She was the oldest grandchild, the oldest child, the oldest cousin, the oldest niece. Myra was only seven when she understood the most basic family fact—there is nothing cute about being the oldest kid. Myra slid into a permanent funk.

My parents didn't handle Myra's decline very well. In fact, they didn't handle it at all. I suspect they didn't notice. I did. I shared a room with Myra. The day she realized that her position in the family had permanently moved from being the sun to being the planet Pluto, Myra divided the room in half. I was only four at the time, but my powers of observation and deduction were already developing. I watched Myra move all her possessions and furniture to her side of the room. I observed as she took a ruler and measured the room before removing all of her hair ribbons from her top dresser drawer. She stretched them flat along some line only she could see. Before stitching them down to the carpet, Myra measured again. When she was through, she looked at me.

"Don't you ever cross this line, Sherelee! That side of the room is yours, this is mine."

Luckily, the door was on my side of the room. "How do you get to the door?" I asked her.

"I can go where I please. I'm the oldest."

"Says who?" I said, sorry immediately.

Myra crossed to where I was sitting and shoved her fist under my nose. "Says me."

For as long as we have shared that room, things have never changed. Myra got her way.

I was sure someone would say something to us after Mom redecorated the whole house. She had our carpet pulled up and a white floor made from some kind of shiny vinyl installed. New furniture arrived and was precisely placed by Mr. Barney, the decorating consultant. He worked from a plan drawn on blueprint paper. When he and Mom were through, the room looked like a display in a department store

4

labeled A Room for the Young Ladies in Your Household.

I sat on my bed, which was right next to Myra's, and wondered what she would do. Myra sat on her bed absolutely silent. We listened to Mr. Barney and our mother coo to each other as they headed for the kitchen to have a cup of coffee. Myra got up, shut the door and began moving furniture. She didn't ask for help. She didn't speak. She just pushed and shoved until all of her things were on her side of the room again. Myra had shoved my new furniture into one corner. I rearranged it as best I could. I was only eight at the time and not that strong. Myra did not offer to help move the heavier pieces.

When I was through, I sat down on my new bed and watched as Myra fished out a new supply of assorted hair ribbons. Then she got out a tube of instant epoxy glue and glued ten feet of ribbon to the floor. I figured our mother was going to kill her. Myra stood up and pushed at a section of ribbon with her toe—it didn't budge. She glared at me. Then she left.

I wondered what Mom would say when she noticed the ribbons glued to the brand-new floor. But she never said anything. Not that day or week or ever. Not a word. It has always amazed me how a family descended from the greatest observer of all time could bumble through life only noticing things they want to notice.

In fact, when Myra finally disappeared, it seemed to my parents that she had vanished suddenly, just like a person in a magic act. I was the only one who had paid any attention to her growing weirdness. For example, the smile. One day Myra came home with this strange smile on her face. It lasted for about an hour, and then her face scrunched into its usual scowl. The next day she came home with the smile again, but it lasted until dinnertime. It went on like that until Myra was getting up in the morning with the smile and going to sleep with it at night. Talk about strange. She was still rotten to me, but at least she smiled when she told me to drop dead.

Then that started to change. She got very polite around the house—even to me. And she started giving me things. "Here, Sherelee, dear, I want you to have my stuffed animal collection." "Sherelee, do you think you might want my posters to hang on your side of the room?" Each time Myra would offer me something, she would pat me on the head and smile that awful smile.

My side of the room filled up with all sorts of junk that used to belong to Myra. Her side of the room got empty—really empty. I started taking note of things of value on Myra's side of the room. Each day, something else would be gone. Myra may have been passing on her worthless stuff to me, but she was taking her good stuff elsewhere. Anything worth money was leaving the room.

I decided to do some detecting.

# 3

I telephoned Watson.

"Why are you getting involved, Sherelee? You don't even like Myra!" Watson whined. "Besides, I'd rather go to the mall."

For once, Watson seemed to make sense. Why was I getting involved? Myra was a jerk. She certainly wouldn't offer to help me if I needed it.

"Also," continued Watson, chittering like a squirrel, "it's probably just your imagination. You know how you are."

That did it. "That does it, Watson!" I shouted into the phone. "After all these years of friendship, all you can manage is the same put-down my family uses. Forget it, Watson. It's over. Go to the mall. Go to the moon. Imagination—bat guano!"

As I hung up the phone, I could hear Watson saying, "Bat what?" I counted to twenty. The phone rang.

"What do you want, Watson?" I hollered into the mouthpiece.

"You're hurting my ears, Sherelee."

"Ear, Watson, ear. You only listen to the phone with one ear."

"Look, I'm sorry I said that about your imagination. I'll come over and help if you still want me to."

While waiting for Watson to arrive, I had a chance to think about my feelings for Myra. My conclusion was that they didn't matter. Great-great-grandpa Sherlock was never bothered by such things. There is no rule that says a detective has to like her clients. If their cause is just and true—that's all that matters.

I then began wondering if Myra could possibly have a just and true cause—or if she could even be one. It was Myra's good fortune that Watson arrived and I was forced to put those thoughts aside.

I sat Watson at my desk with a large yellow pad and a pen.

"Make notes," I said, opening Myra's closet.

"What kind of notes?"

"Notes we can read later. Write down what I tell you."

"What are you going to do, Sherelee? That's Myra's closet." Watson's whine went up a few notes. She was getting nervous.

"Of course it's Myra's closet. I'm looking for clues."

"She's going to kill us. This is snooping."

"No it isn't, it's detecting. Relax. Myra won't be home for hours, Watson. Just take the notes and stop whining."

"I'm not whining," she whined. Watson has always whined. It gets worse when she is nervous, bored or frightened. Her nickname in school is Siren.

7

"And for the record," Watson added, "see, I'm even writing it down—my name is Watkins. *K-I-N-S*. Joan Watkins. And I am NOT involved in any of this. OK."

"Fine," I said. I methodically searched Myra's half of our room, carefully replacing each thing exactly where I found it. I had Watson make a list of what I discovered—like missing coats and shoes and the absence of Myra's radio, stereo, camera and all her jewelry. It was worse than I had expected. Even most of Myra's T-shirts and much of her underwear were missing. I was puzzled. Search completed, I pulled Myra's desk chair next to Watson and studied the list.

"Maybe she's selling things and buying drugs," offered Watson.

"It's good to see you putting your mind to the case, Watson —but underwear—and T-shirts and shoes? No, I am sure this is not drug-related."

"Watkins."

"Whatever."

Watson jumped to her feet. "That's it, Sherelee. I wish I had gone to the mall. This is stupid. Probably all Myra's things are in the laundry—or at the cleaners. Maybe she lent her other stuff to friends—and it's Watkins, Watkins, WAT-KINS! I have been Joan Watkins all of my life—right up until you decided you were the great-granddaughter of Sherlock Holmes."

"Great-GREAT-granddaughter. Now sit down and I'll tell you what I have concluded."

Watson sat. Even she had some curiosity.

"Myra is about to leave this family. If you observe carefully, the only things of value left on her side of the room are her typewriter and desk lamp. This is serious, Watson. We are going to have to take action."

Watson got very pale. "I have to go home now. There's an after-school special on TV I have to see. For social studies class." Watson was backing toward the door. I never should have mentioned the word *action*.

"TELEVISION? My sister's very life may be in danger, and you are going home to watch television? What kind of a Watson are you, anyway?"

"I'm a WATKINS Watson, that's what kind!" Watson ran out of the room. I heard the front door slam.

Alone, I stared at the list. I was beginning to see there was a pattern. If I was right about what it meant, Myra was just about gone.

I was absolutely certain that Myra was not capable of being as sneaky and efficient as she had been those past few weeks. Someone had to be coaching her. Who was the fiend? What had Myra gotten involved in? Why did she smile all of the time? Where had she taken her socks and underwear and other clothing?

There was only one thing I could do. My decision was made. I would follow Myra. I would do it the next day before she disappeared along with the last of her possessions.

# 4

That night I ate my dinner so fast that even my mother noticed. I must have set a world speed-eating record. My stomach hurt, so I didn't mind missing dessert. I asked to be excused and left the table before my parents had gotten halfway through their meatloaf. There was too much to think about, and I needed quiet.

I went to my room and lay down on my bed. Relaxation helps the brain to function better. The situation with Myra was critical. It was already Wednesday. I calculated that

Myra would disappear along with the last valuable item on her side of the room. What was left were her lamp and typewriter.

The lamp was a fairly large antique—ugly but costly. Figuring that Myra couldn't possibly carry both things without dropping one, I deduced that she would leave Friday. Unless, of course, she was planning to steal other things from the house. If that were the case, she would stay awhile, and I would have more time to find out what was going on.

But I couldn't take a chance. I had to count on Friday being D-Day—Disappearance Day—or I might lose track of her. I needed a plan.

The first fact I had to confront about the case was that my being a kid detective created all sorts of unique problems. For example, I did not have complete freedom of movement. I was expected to go to school each day and to go to bed at a reasonable hour at night. I thought about what Great-great-grandpa Sherlock might do in my place.

I decided to cut school for the rest of the week. Sometimes detectives find it necessary to break certain rules in order to pursue their profession. No one in my family would notice my planned absence unless the school called my house.

The second thing I decided was that since I was still technically a kid—that is to say, I looked like a kid, was as tall as a kid and had a kid's voice—it would be impossible for me to use some of Great-great-grandpa's most effective detecting techniques.

Great-great-grandpa Sherlock was a master of disguises. When on a case, he was able to change his appearance so he could blend in anywhere and spy on his suspects and enemies. He could appear to be any kind of person in the world.

Great-great-grandpa Sherlock had a closetful of costumes and drawers filled with stage makeup, false noses, putty, wigs and beards. I, on the other hand, had a box leftover from Halloween. In it were a half jar of green skin paint, false

10

purple fingernails, a black witch wig and a large plastic nose with eyeglasses and a mustache attached to it.

There was no way that I, a person who looked exactly as old as she was, could wear any of that stuff so that I could anonymously blend in anywhere. As a matter of fact, I think that even Great-great-grandpa might have had some trouble using what I had on hand. I was going to have to follow Myra looking like myself. I would have to depend upon my skill as a professional shadow. I would have to slip in and out of alleys and doorways so Myra wouldn't notice me.

I hated to do it, but I telephoned Watson again. I needed help.

"Watson, I need your help. It's urgent!"

"Oh, Sherelee," she whined, "I don't want to get in trouble." Watson usually responds to cries for help in this way.

"Listen, Watson, I swear you won't get into trouble."

"Are you sure, Sherelee?" she pleaded. Then Watson got cagey. "If I do whatever it is you're going to ask, I want to go back to being Joan Watkins." The whine almost left her voice.

"You are a most unsatisfactory detecting colleague, Watson—however, I agree," I lied. People who bribe other people should not expect honesty in return.

"OK. What do you want me to do?"

"Meet me at six forty-five tomorrow morning in my backyard. Come the old way—through the fences."

"That's so early. Can't we do it later? I don't have to leave for school until eight thirty. What will I tell my mother? What if I tear my clothing on the fences?" Watson's whine was almost a squeal.

"You promised, Watson. Don't ask questions. Don't come through the front yards. Don't let anyone see you. Wear old clothing if you're worried. The whole favor will only take ten minutes. Is that too much to ask?" I sounded very firm.

"I don't know. What if I get caught? What if . . ." I

11

slammed down the phone. Then I counted to twenty. Naturally it rang. Watson is predictable.

"Sherelee? I promised, so I'll do it. I'll be there at six forty-five."

"Good. And don't forget the note."

"What note? You didn't say anything about a note."

"Didn't I? It's the note you're going to write—the one addressed to Mrs. Corwin, my homeroom teacher, explaining how you are taking me away on important family business for two days. Sign my mother's name. Mrs. Corwin won't recognize your handwriting."

Watson made a horrible screeching noise. "Nooooooooooo, Sherelee. They'll find out. I'll get detention for a year."

"Don't be a wimp, Watson. Just write the note and meet me. I have to go. I've got plans to make."

I hung up the phone before Watson could change her mind. I knew she would do as I asked. It was exactly ten o'clock. Watson would rather be boiled in oil than telephone someone's house on a weeknight after ten o'clock. She was terrified she might disturb a sleeping member of the family and get hollered at. In addition, Watson is a loyal person and wouldn't think of letting me down without warning me first. Watson would write the note.

Being a great detective requires that you understand the psychology of the people around you.

# 5

"Here, Sherelee, take it!" Watson scowled as she waved the note in front of my nose. It was written on pale blue, expensive stationery.

"Nice touch, Watson, taking some of your mother's good paper to do the job."

Watson winced. "I'm going to get caught. Don't you even want to look at it? I was up half the night making it perfect." I grabbed the note from her hand the next time it passed by my face, read it and handed it back.

Watson had done a superior job. The writing looked just like the casual, offhanded writing of a busy adult.

"Good show, Watson, but I'm in a big hurry. I can't stand around exchanging pleasantries. Now take my schoolbooks home with you and hide them in your room. I'll pick them up later today."

"You're beginning to talk more and more like one of those Sherlock Holmes books, Sherelee. Where are you going, anyway?" Watson seemed to be settling in for a social visit. Sizing up the situation, I ignored her comment and responded to her question.

"I can't tell you. The less you know, the safer you'll be."

Since Watson has always been more concerned for her own safety than for anything else in this world, my words seemed to spin her around and push her toward home—at a run. As she went through the bushes, I called after her, "Put the note in a matching envelope, Watson." I could hear her whimper, but she did not stop for even a second.

I was relieved. At that point, my plans were very vague indeed. I had no idea of where I might wind up that day, and it is never a good idea for a detective to admit uncertainty. It destroys confidence.

I had left a note for my mother telling her there was an early-morning meeting at school of a club I wanted to join. Myra always left for school at seven thirty, and I had to be positioned in a place where I could see her and follow her. I was wearing dungarees, a sweatshirt, a baseball cap and sneakers. I looked like any anonymous kid. I think Great-

great-grandpa would have been proud of me. My short hair and my carefully chosen nondisguise would enable me to blend in just about anywhere in town. In fact, with the cap pulled down over my face, you couldn't even tell if I was male or female. No one would notice me—I hoped.

As soon as Watson was out of sight, I slipped through our front yard and onto the street. I chose a disintegrating wooden fence surrounding a deserted old house to hide behind. It was centrally located on the block. I could peek through the broken slats and see our front door, and no one could spot me from behind. The fence provided perfect cover for surveillance.

According to my digital watch, Myra marched out of the house at exactly 7:32. She walked toward State Street. She appeared to be going to school. Her books were under one arm, and she carried what looked like my black raincoat—the one with all the pockets and the belt and the shoulder tabs—under her other arm. I almost forgot my mission and ran out to grab it from her. I loved that raincoat. When I wore it, I looked like a professional detective—or a spy. It took a great deal of mental discipline, but I stopped myself just in time.

I casually stepped onto the sidewalk and walked behind Myra. She was about three-quarters of a block in front of me. I could see that the raincoat bunched under her arm looked strangely awkward and bulky. It was obvious, she had my coat wrapped around her desk lamp. She was ruining my detective coat. I could only hope that Myra would have the decency to return it once she had delivered the lamp.

State Street is a busy thoroughfare. Once on it, I was afraid Myra would do something radical, like suddenly jumping on a public bus. She turned the corner. I hurried to catch up to her. Just as I rounded the corner, I saw Myra step up to a parked car, open the back door and put the coat/lamp package on the back seat. She then leaned in the front window, said

14

a few words to the driver, slammed the rear door and proceeded down the street. I tried to hurry so I could see the driver's face before he pulled away, but he was too fast for me.

However, I was able to identify the make of the car and record the license plate in my small detecting notepad. The car was a very new-looking Rolls-Royce. The license plate had the inscription PERFECT 3 on it.

I had been wondering if Myra would try to jam the antique lamp into her school locker or carry it around with her all day. It even crossed my mind that she might skip school to deliver it. I was not expecting her to give it to someone who was driving a car which cost around $120,000.

Who was he? What did he need with Myra's desk lamp? Had she given all of her things to him—including her socks, underwear and T-shirts? What kind of weirdo was he—was she, for that matter? Was I wrong? Was he some strange kind of drug pusher—his car was certainly expensive.

The rest of the walk to the high school was uneventful. By the time the eight o'clock bell rang, Myra was in the building and, I presumed, in class. I would have plenty of time to decide what to do next. I had six hours to lurk and think.

# 6

If you are a kid, lurking around a high school isn't all that hard. You have plenty of company. Even at a strict school like State Street High, kids sneak out during study halls to smoke cigarettes or to buy soda or food at the stores across the street.

I moved from one store to another each time a period bell rang so no single merchant would get angry and draw attention to me by ordering me into the street. Storekeepers are kinder to customers, so whenever I entered a new store, I bought a small drink or snack. I spent a sizable piece of my allowance buying goodwill.

I kept a record of my expenses in my notebook. If I managed to save Myra from whatever it was she needed saving from, I intended to bill my parents.

Myra did not leave the school during the day, but the last bell was still ringing when she rushed out the side door near the gym. I was ready for her because I had been able to sneak a look at her schedule the night before. I was actually crossing the street, heading toward the gym door, when Myra appeared. I pulled the cap low over my eyes. Myra passed no more than three feet from me. She was grinning that stupid grin, and her eyes were kind of staring at nothing. I think I could have walked right next to her, and she wouldn't have known it was me.

At the bus stop, Myra dug into her purse. Luckily, I still had some money left for my own fare. I got on the bus a few people behind Myra and turned my head away when I passed where she was sitting. There were no seats left where I could easily see her, so I stood. The bus filled up with high school kids, and, short as I am, I had a hard time keeping her in sight. I worked my way to the rear door. I wanted to be able to jump off the bus without delay. At each stop, I pushed my head through the crowd to see if Myra was getting off. I was almost decapitated twice. I really hope I grow a few inches before I am forced to attend school with those lummoxes.

We rode for a long time. The bus emptied. Now I was sure I would be spotted. I sat down and slumped as low as I could. Then, about two stops from the end of the line, in the busiest part of town, Myra got off the bus. I followed.

It was easy to shadow her through the crowded downtown streets, even though she was walking very fast. Without warning, Myra turned into a store. She didn't come out. I looked at the beautifully painted sign over the doorway. NEARLY

16

PERFECT SHOPPE. I sauntered up to the window, cap low, hand sort of casually covering my face. I could see Myra talking to the people behind the counter of the store. The store seemed to have a little bit of everything. Then I noticed the small, tasteful sign in the corner of the window: ELEGANT, FINE, NEARLY PERFECT, ALMOST NEW MERCHANDISE. A PLACE FOR THE SHOPPER WITH DISCRETION.

It was a secondhand store! What was Myra doing here? I pretended to be looking at things in the window. Customers were going in and out. Myra disappeared into the back of the store and reappeared wearing light blue coveralls. She began dusting items on the shelves. Did Myra have a job? The Myra I knew wouldn't wash a dish unless under threat of life imprisonment.

All the employees were wearing blue clothing, although Myra was the only one in coveralls. And they were smiling. They grinned at customers, each other, the racks of clothing, the cash register—a seemingly happy bunch of people. Why was I so bothered by them? My brain began fitting pieces of information together—like a very slow computer. I had a moment of apprehension about all the sugar I had eaten that day. Maybe I had damaged my finely tuned brain cells. I began to get a funny feeling in the pit of my stomach. I knew I had the key somewhere in my memory, but I just couldn't find it.

There was a lull in the street traffic. Shoppers had left the store. Standing in front of the Nearly Perfect Shoppe was getting awkward. I was bound to be noticed. I was afraid that Myra would break out of her smiling fog just long enough to see me hanging around. If I was recognized, all would be lost. I was about to walk away when I saw all the people in blue —and Myra—stop what they were doing, turn to a photograph on the wall, close their eyes and bow from the waist. I looked at my watch. It was three thirty.

That was as strange a sight as I had ever seen. Also terrifying, because suddenly all the information that had been rattling around in my head came together. I remembered what I had heard about the Nearly Perfect Shoppe. It was owned by the Temple of Perfection, and the Temple of Perfection was a cult. Myra was in much worse trouble than I had guessed.

I wandered back and forth on the block, watching the entrance. At four o'clock, Myra, wearing her school clothes and carrying her books, stepped onto the sidewalk. A woman in a long, light blue dress followed her out of the store and hugged her. As Myra walked toward the bus, the woman called after her, "Only until tomorrow, Little Sister. Have patience."

I felt a shiver work its way up my spine. Poor, dumb Myra. What had she gotten herself into? I wished Great-great-grandpa were around to talk to. He would have had some brilliant ideas about what to do next. I took a deep breath and made a quick decision. It was obvious that Myra would have to go home, because the typewriter was still there. Besides, the woman in blue indicated that tomorrow was the big day. So, instead of following Myra, I let her get out of sight and wandered into the store. It was very fancy for a secondhand store. Things actually did look new. Other shoppers had come in, and I felt a little out of place among the very well-dressed people. However, no one seemed to mind my being there.

"Can I help you, dear?" It was the same woman who had hugged Myra. She was smiling Myra's smile.

"No, thank you. I'm just looking around, if that's OK with you."

"Certainly it is. Would you like a cold drink or something to eat?"

"No, thank you. I'm not hungry."

"Oh. Do you live in town here?"

"Yes, I do."

"In that case, I'll leave you alone. Here in the Place of Perfect Peace we are always looking for poor runaways to take in and nurture. If you need help, please call me or any of the other Sisters or Brothers—anytime." She gave me what I guessed she thought was a meaningful look. She had also given me the information I had been seeking . . . and a case of the creeps.

The woman was obviously a cult recruiter. I felt as if I were being lured by one of those jungle plants that attracts flies with sweet nectar. When the fly enters the flower of the plant, it gets trapped. The plant then eats the fly. I wanted to get out of there, but I had to finish my investigation.

I wandered around the Nearly Perfect Shoppe, making mental note of everything in it. Sure enough, there was the desk lamp. I thought I recognized Myra's stereo. It was difficult picking out her radio and tape recorder because there were so many—all looking new.

I figured I would have better luck with the clothing. The racks and shelves were as neat as racks and shelves in a boutique. Everything was arranged by size. I could positively identify only two of Myra's dresses and her just-bought spring jacket.

Then I came across my coat. My wonderful black coat. Someone must have ironed it, because there wasn't a wrinkle in either sleeve. I couldn't help myself. I took it off the hanger and put it on. I buttoned the buttons. I buckled the belt. I stood in front of the full-length mirror. I turned up the collar.

"It fits you perfectly, dear. It's as if it were made for you." I looked at the smiling, skinny, nervous man in the blue shirt. Only a great detective could have kept as calm as I did.

"It's very nice," I said.

"Wear it for a while, child. It's a real bargain. It's quite new —hardly been worn. It's just come into the shop today."

I could have made a scene. I could have called in a policeman. I could have telephoned my parents and had them come to the store and make a scene, but I suspected that none of that would help Myra. She would be accused of being a thief. My parents would drag Myra home and ground her. Myra would hate us even more than she already did. At the first opportunity, she would run away and be pulled further into the cult. No, I had to be cool. Detectives sometimes have to make sacrifices.

I took off the coat, hung it on the hanger, explained to the man that it wasn't a matter of price—the coat just wasn't right for me—and left the shop. As I passed the glass counter-case, I caught a glimpse of Myra's gold heart pendant. Myra was earning the Temple of Perfection a bundle of money—and as far as I could tell, she wasn't even quite an official member. That would happen tomorrow. Time had run out.

# 7

All the way home, I tried to decide which would be the best action to take. If I simply went to my parents with the news, Myra would think that I had maliciously betrayed her. First, she would get even—probably by punching me—then, most likely, she would just take off in the night. Nothing would be accomplished. On the other hand, talking directly to Myra would present problems. We had never, in my memory, had a conversation. Never. When I pictured myself talking to Myra, I felt tongue-tied. It had nothing to do with the touchy subject matter. It had everything to do with being told to shut up for most of my life.

I thought about what Great-great-grandpa Sherlock might do. He was a very straightforward fellow. He would never have gone behind someone's back to rat on her. He would have confronted the situation head-on. I knew in my heart that if he were sitting beside me on the bus, Great-great-grandpa would advise me to talk to Myra. He would tell me to present her with such dazzling reasoning that the last thing she would want to do in the world would be to join the Temple of Perfection.

It was decided. I ran home from the bus stop. Myra was in our room. As I walked in, she shoved something under her bed. I noticed that her dresser drawers were open. I looked in the closet. Myra's overnight bag was not hanging on its usual hook. I had probably interrupted her final packing.

There was no polite or easy way to begin the conversation. We had never talked, so there was no way to lead up to the topic casually. For example, I couldn't very well say, "Myra, I've been wondering—do you know anything about cults?" First of all, the sound of my voice in our room would startle her. Second, my asking her opinion about anything—no matter how ordinary and inconsequential I made it sound— would be so out of character that she would instantly become suspicious and defensive.

So I went straight to the point. "Myra, I saw you going into the Nearly Perfect Shoppe today."

Myra turned around and smiled at me.

"You did? How nice."

I took a deep breath and continued. "I know you've been taking things out of the house and giving them to the Temple of Perfection. I saw you in the store dusting and working, and I saw you bow to that picture. I even heard what that woman said to you. I know you're planning to run away and join the Temple tomorrow." I refrained from mentioning my raincoat —I didn't want to appear hostile.

Not that it mattered. Myra's smile seemed to freeze on

her face. Her eyes got squinty, and her voice sounded slippery and mean. I suddenly felt as if I were talking to a snake. "Well, well, Little Sister"—she practically spat out the words *little sister*—"you certainly have been busy prying into my life. Have you told any of this to your mother and father yet?"

"OUR mother and father, Myra. No, I haven't. I thought you and I could talk about this in a reasonable manner first. There's no need to drag them into it, especially if you decide not to go."

"Decide NOT to go? I warn you, Sherelee, butt out of my life. If you try to stop me, the BROTHERHOOD will take care of you. Do you understand what I am saying?"

"You're threatening me, right? Why don't we just calmly and rationally discuss this major decision of yours like two human beings who care about each other—like family." I looked kindly at Myra, trying to project nonthreatening warmth and caring. She glared at me.

"Go stuff an eggplant up your nose. No one in this house is in MY family." Myra's smile was gone. There was nothing in her face that told me she recognized me as a blood relative —a sister. She stared at me for at least a minute and then did the one thing I was positive she would not do. Myra opened her mouth and yelled, "MOTHER!" She then went out the door of our room and headed toward the den. As she moved, her cries changed from "Mother! Mother!" to "MOMMY! MOMMY!" It sounded as if someone were killing her and she was desperately calling for help. I was sure that by the time she reached the den, big, sad tears would be dripping down her face. This was not going according to plan.

Sensing disaster, I followed my former big sister. It was just one more time in my life when I wished with all my heart that Great-great-grandpa Sherlock had left behind a manual of specific instructions to be used in emergencies.

22

# 8

When I reached the den, Myra was in the middle of an hysterical fit. She was kneeling in front of my mother's chair, sobbing and blathering. Mother was wiping Myra's tears away with a handkerchief and patting Myra on the back in a comforting manner.

My mother leaned forward and put her arms around Myra. Myra actually lifted her lip and sneered at me. I had never seen a human do that in real life. Then she sat back and looked tearfully and lovingly at my mother. It was a great performance. I got that awful sinking feeling you get in your stomach when you realize things are hopeless.

For the first time in years, Myra held the attention of our entire small family. Even my father turned off the television news to listen to her rave. Myra went from passion to pity—from tears of pain to small smiles of love—from protests of her innocence to accusations regarding my sanity and truthfulness.

She began with the statement, "She's making me crazy. Please make her stop. PLEASE. She's hounding me. She's ruining my life. Please help me." I, of course, was the *she* in this speech.

Myra accused me of being a snoop. She admitted being at the Nearly Perfect Shoppe but said she went there to buy my mother a birthday present, because they had nice inexpensive things and she was broke. Then Myra made a long statement about my needing a psychiatrist because of my detective obsession.

I was allowed to say nothing. NOTHING. My parents

forced me to stand and listen to the incredible lies. Finally, when the three of them voted to ground ME for a month, I blew my top.

"Isn't anyone going to ask me MY side? What is this, a kangaroo court? Why are you asking Myra if grounding me for a month is fair? What about her joining the Temple of Perfection? Why don't you go check her side of our room? Everything expensive is missing. All her clothing is gone. She's getting ready to leave—take a powder—do a bunk. DO YOU UNDERSTAND ME?"

I was shouting. I wasn't being calmly logical. I wasn't presenting a good case. Myra saw her opportunity, threw herself onto my father's lap and cried. She put her whole heart into it. Her shoulders shook, she had trouble catching her breath, huge tears rolled off her face and wet the front of his shirt.

My father held Myra and lectured me. He said Myra had been sweet, helpful and cheerful during the past number of weeks. He said that those weren't the symptoms of an unhappy kid who was about to run away. My father said he didn't know what was bothering me, but I was well aware of the family rule against prying into the business of others. I was to go to my room and leave my sister alone. Or else.

I knew when to retreat. Somehow I had horribly miscalculated the scope of Myra's cunning and devious nature. As a consequence, Myra was going off to join the cult—unobstructed. I couldn't physically hold her. My parents probably could have but wouldn't because they didn't believe me.

I had forgotten to pick up my books from Watson's house, so I sat at my desk with a volume of the encyclopedia and pretended to take notes. What I was really doing was making a list of plans. Myra came in, took her overnight bag from under her bed and finished packing. She put the typewriter in its case. There was no reason for her to hide anything from me now. As for our parents, she was as sure as I was that they would make a special effort to avoid even glancing into our room that night.

Myra didn't say a word to me. After a while, I went to take a bath. When I returned, Myra was in bed with her face to the wall. I turned out the light.

"Myra, are you sure you know what you are doing? People in cults like the Temple of Perfection are—"

"If you don't shut up, Sherelee, I'm going to go to your father and do the crying bit all over again."

I believed her. I shut up. I continued making plans in my head.

# 9

I woke up knowing exactly what I would have to do. First, it was absolutely necessary that I ignore being grounded. Second, I had to get out of the house before Myra. I pried open my treasure-chest bank and stuffed about three dollars' worth of change into my pockets. This was getting to be a very expensive case. I grabbed the emergency candy bar which was hidden in my bottom desk drawer and left via the back door. As I had the day before, I waited behind the broken fence.

Myra left the house fifteen minutes early. Mother waved to her from the door, not seeming to notice the overnight bag hanging on Myra's shoulder or the typewriter in its case, which kept bumping against Myra's leg. As for Myra, she actually skipped down the street despite the load she was carrying. This was her big day.

After Mother went inside, I eased myself onto the street and began following Myra. It was a short day's work. Myra

25

rounded the corner, set down the typewriter and the suitcase and leaned against a telephone pole. I slouched behind a big maple trying to look natural. We waited for exactly thirteen minutes. A big Rolls-Royce slid next to the curb. It was identical to the one the day before, but the license plate said PERFECT 2.

A man in a chauffeur's cap was driving. A woman sat in the backseat. Myra opened the door and handed the typewriter to her. Then she leaned into the car, and it looked to me as if she took the woman's hand and touched it to her forehead.

The car pulled away from the curb as the door closed. Myra waved and smiled. I got ready to begin tailing her again, but instead of moving, Myra just stood there with that stupid grin on her face. I looked at my watch. I looked at Myra. She remained immobile for exactly ten and a half minutes.

Foot traffic was getting pretty heavy with people heading toward school and work. It was getting difficult for me to look like I belonged scrunched up against a tree. I couldn't take the chance and change my stakeout position, because I had no idea what Myra might do next. What if she took off while I was busily finding a less conspicuous place to hide? I ignored the funny looks I was starting to get from passersby. Then a horrible racket moved up the street toward us, diverting all attention from me. It sounded like a boiler exploding.

Everyone stopped and watched as a decrepit bright blue van belched its way up State Street. When it was opposite where Myra stood, it did a U-turn—forcing traffic to screech to a halt in both directions. The rest happened very fast. The van slowed down to a crawl, the back doors opened and hands reached out and lifted Myra in as the van pulled away from the curb. Before the doors shut, I could see that there were about five other people in the small truck. They were surrounded by bunches of artificial-looking flowers. They were

26

all smiling. I stepped out from behind the tree to get a better look, but the doors were pulled shut. All I saw were the bright gold foot-high letters—TOP PARADISE EXPRESS.

It was seven forty-five in the morning, and Myra was already gone. She had been whisked away to Temple of Perfection Paradise—wherever that was. However, I had counted on this very kind of catastrophe happening. No villain would ever again catch this Holmes off guard and totally unprepared.

The night before, I had realized that Myra was going to disappear from our family no matter what I did. I therefore switched the emphasis of my job from prevention to rescue. I wasn't expecting her to take off from a street corner right near our house, but it hardly mattered. I had investigating to do. I pulled out my notepad and looked at my list of plans.

On the bus downtown, I ate my emergency candy bar. Sugar in the morning generally makes me a little sick, but I was trying to conserve funds by not buying breakfast. There was a lot I had to do before going home—a cash reserve might prove useful.

# 10

The Nearly Perfect Shoppe was closed when I arrived. I noted the store hours posted on the door and proceeded to wander around downtown. There was nothing special I wanted to do or see—I just didn't want to appear to be anxiously awaiting the arrival of the Temple of Perfection people. At nine forty-five, I showed up at the store. The same smiling woman in blue was dusting the shelves. No matter what else can be said about the Temple of Perfection, they probably run

27

the cleanest thrift shop in the United States—maybe the world.

"Hello, dear. You're back again. Have you come to buy that nice coat you tried on yesterday?"

"No. I have several very nice coats at home. I'm bored with coats," I lied.

"Really? Well then, shouldn't you be in school now?"

"I didn't feel like going today. It's boring." I began getting into character by sighing a bored sigh and letting my mouth hang open a bit while tilting my head back and staring at the ceiling. The effect was wasted on the woman, because she never looked up from her dusting.

"Won't your parents be upset when the school notifies them of your absence?" She sounded as if she were reciting memorized questions that she had asked a thousand times before.

I sat down on a stool and stared at the color photo they had all bowed to the day before. In it was a grim-faced man with a neatly trimmed, blue black pointed beard and a large drooping mustache. Both were outlined by a fringe of white hair. He glowered at the camera. The effect was absolutely weird —he looked as if he came from another planet.

The blue-bearded man wore a brilliant blue suit. Its color was the only cheerful thing about him. He looked as if he had never smiled in his life. His eyes were black and penetrating. His eyebrows were very thick—blue black with that same white fringe. They arched over his eyes in perfect, neat half-moons. All in all, he was the meanest, toughest, nastiest-looking man I had ever seen. He also looked smart. I studied his face and thought about Myra. If that was who I thought it was, this case was going to prove more difficult than I had anticipated.

During my examination of the photo, the woman had continued to dust the merchandise. She seemed to be operating on some kind of automatic pilot. I had to get her attention. She had asked the crucial question without knowing it—the key to my plan. I had no idea it would come up so early in the conversation. I answered slowly so I'd be sure she actually heard what I said.

"Nope. The school won't tell my parents. They'll let my lawyers know, and I'll just make some excuse. And the lawyers—well, they don't really care what I do as long as I stay out of their way."

She stopped dusting. I kept looking at the picture. "Your lawyers? Where are your parents?"

"Dead. Died in a skydiving accident three years ago. It's just me and my lawyers—until I'm eighteen, of course." I continued my lie.

The woman in blue pulled over a stool and sat down next to me. I stopped looking at the photograph and stared her straight in the eyes. When you look someone straight in the eyes, that person usually decides you are telling the truth. She seemed very excited about my misfortune.

"You poor dear. What's your name?"

"Cynthia." I had decided beforehand to lie about my name. On the bus I had practiced making my new name sound natural. Then I completed it for the woman who was now patting me sympathetically on the arm. "Cynthia Vanderbelt."

"Vanderbilt?" The woman practically choked getting the name out. Her eyes were watering with excitement. "THE Vanderbilt family?"

"No, VanderBELT. It's a lesser-known, but older name." I left that vague enough so she would be slightly confused yet too embarrassed to ask detailed questions. Some people think they should be familiar with the intimate lives of famous rich people. Fortunately, she was such a person.

"Well, you poor child, what brings you back to our little store?"

I tried to sound as arrogant as I could—as if I had been rich and bored and spoiled my entire life. "The one thing I am

NOT is poor. All I have is money. I can't tell you how tired I am of shopping for things. I have a house, a boat, two horses and three servants to take care of everything, but it all stinks." I looked at the picture on the wall again. "Who's he and who are you?"

"That's THE Most Important Person in the World. That's a picture of our Sainted and Beloved Daddy Perfect, Leader of The Brotherhood." She looked at the photograph and bobbed her head in a little bow.

"What's The Brotherhood?" I asked, using the same kind of emphasis she had used.

"It's all the people who belong to the Temple of Perfection. It's a loving society of men and women and boys and girls. It's a Spiritual Brotherhood founded by Daddy Perfect. It's . . ." her voice trailed off. A man in a dark blue shirt and light blue pants came through the back door.

"Oh, Brother Robert, I'm so glad to see you." The woman dragged Brother Robert into a corner where she whispered furiously. I tried not to look interested. After a few minutes, I got up, stretched and wandered toward the front door.

They were at my side in a flash. "Sister AP Wendy took the liberty of telling me your name. Let me introduce myself to you, Cynthia. I am Brother Robert. Brother Perfect Robert."

"Sister AP Wendy?"

"Almost Perfect."

"Almost Perfect?" I replied.

"It has to do with The Brotherhood. We can't really explain it to you . . . yet." Brother Robert took a long pause between *you* and *yet* and looked at me in what I guess he thought was a sad and kindly manner. Actually, he looked as if he were about to throw up. I took a step backward just in case. Brother Robert thought I was leaving. He reached out and grabbed my arm.

"Might we offer you some refreshment—a cold drink, a sandwich, a piece of cake?"

I looked at my watch and then at the ceiling and the walls and, finally, at Brother Perfect Robert. A fine line of perspiration had formed on his upper lip. His hand on my arm was trembling slightly. I decided to put the man out of his misery.

"Why not, Brother Perfect Robert? I am getting a bit hungry."

"Brother Robert or BP Robert might be easier for you to say." He smiled and let go of my arm.

"Swell," I said and followed BP Robert and AP Wendy toward the door at the back of the store.

# 11

BP Robert and I sat at a small table while Sister AP Wendy prepared food. Nothing was said while she banged the refrigerator door, rattled knives and forks and clanked dishes. BP's body blocked my line of sight, so I couldn't see what AP Wendy was making. I was sure it would be something pretty elaborate. For about fifteen minutes, BP simply sat with his hands folded on the table, staring at the wall behind me and smiling. It was creepy. I had to keep reminding myself that I was on a case. I cleared my throat a couple of times to get BP's attention, but he just shook his head and continued to smile and stare.

I was in a tricky spot and couldn't afford to make a single mistake. I sat back and waited. Finally, Sister AP whirled around to face us. In her hands was a large dish covered by a paper napkin. She set the dish down in the middle of the table and bobbed her head. "Perfect Praise to our Perfect Daddy." Then she whisked the napkin off the dish with a flourish and stood back smiling.

BP Robert waved his hands over the dish and said, "Praise

Daddy." Then he picked up one of the peanut butter and jelly sandwiches and put it on my plate. "Nice work, Sister AP Wendy," he said. "You may eat with us."

AP Wendy smiled so hard she practically cried with joy. She took one of the sandwiches and stood by the sink eating it. BP looked at me and managed to smile while he ate. He didn't seem to be having the same trouble I was having. I wasn't able to get the white bread, peanut butter and jelly out of my mouth and into my throat. Sister AP hadn't offered us anything to drink. I noticed that she wasn't having any trouble either.

"May I please have something to drink?" I asked, slowly forcing my tongue away from the roof of my mouth where it seemed glued.

BP Robert spoke. "During off-hour meals, we in The Brotherhood only drink after we eat, but since you are as yet an outsider, you may have a beverage." He wiggled his finger at AP, and she managed to get me a drink in under five minutes. It was the stickiest, cheapest cola I had ever tasted. I drank it anyway. I had to get the goo down.

"You must be wondering why we did not talk while Sister AP was preparing our meal," said BP. I nodded. He continued, "Our beloved DP teaches us that the preparation of food is a sacred act and that our women should never confuse themselves with worldly distractions while participating in such holiness."

"DP? Your women?"

"DP is the way we sometimes refer to Daddy Perfect, Our Teacher. He has taught us that it is women who must cook the meals. It is their Sacred Place."

I gagged. I pretended I was choking on my sandwich—a logical possibility. I was on a case. I said this to myself about ten times in my head while I spit a mouthful of goop into my napkin. Then I looked up sweetly and said, "How interesting."

Sister AP Wendy bobbed and bowed and milled about, dusting the kitchen, washing the dishes, but she never quite took her eyes off BP Robert. When he twitched his finger, she was at his side asking what was needed. When she failed to respond instantly, BP shook his head and frowned, and Sister AP's eyes would fill with tears. She was positively slavelike.

BP Robert did most of the talking. He asked me questions about school and my interests, which I answered vaguely and in as few words as possible. I volunteered nothing. When I finally finished the last bite of my sandwich, I yawned and looked at my watch. This made BP more nervous—which is what I wanted. He abruptly got to the point.

"It must be rough on you being an orphan."

"Not really. Mostly it's boring . . ." I looked down at the floor and in a small voice added, "and lonely." You would have thought I had just dropped a pound of gold in BP's lap. These were the words he had been waiting for.

"Lonely. LONELY! No one is ever lonely in The Brotherhood. The Brotherhood is love. The Brotherhood is Family. The BROTHERHOOD is PERFECTION!"

BP Robert went on and on. As he talked, he got more and more excited. His waved his arms and tossed his head. He even forgot to smile. His voice got louder, and his eyes focused on some far-off place. Then, without warning, he simply stopped. He wasn't at the end of a particular point he was making or even at the end of a thought. He just stopped. Sister AP Wendy beamed at him and brought him a cold glass of cola.

After a few minutes of smiling silence, I looked at my watch.

"I have to go home now." They appeared to be disappointed. BP signaled to Sister AP Wendy, and she pulled some pamphlets out of a drawer and handed them to me.

"These will explain some things about The Brotherhood. We will be here to answer any questions you might have. Here

33

is our special telephone number." Sister AP handed me a business card with a telephone number printed under the words PERFECTION IS POSSIBLE.

I folded the pamphlets around the card and stuffed it all into my pocket. I turned to go.

"Wait." It was BP.

"May I give you a lift somewhere? Anywhere?"

"Why not?" I said. "I'm going home." It was working. My plan was working. I was too good a catch for them to just let me wander off into the street. Great-great-grandpa Sherlock would have been so proud of me.

"Where do you live?" We were walking toward a large, black Lincoln sedan. Brother Perfect Robert was doing well in The Brotherhood, but he wasn't at the top of things. I wondered who got to drive around in the Rolls-Royces.

"Harbor Heights. Vista Drive. Number 3." I named the most exclusive street in the most exclusive neighborhood in town. BP was impressed. He held open the back door of the car for me, and I got in. Sister AP did not come along.

It took about fifteen minutes to get to Vista Drive. During the ride, I thought about how often luck and chance contribute to success. It just so happened that my godparents, Mo and Flo Vogel, were one of the richest couples in town— maybe in the state. Flo had been my mother's roommate in college. When she married Mo, they discovered that they had a talent for speculating in something called the commodities market. They made a fortune in pork belly futures—at least that's what my parents told me. Sometimes I don't know if I'm being told the truth about things. In the case of pig stomachs and their futures, I don't care.

Flo and Mo are nice people. They have no kids of their own, but they have always given Myra and me the run of their house and grounds—even when they were away on vacation —which they were when Myra disappeared.

I'm not sure I could have bluffed my way through the

rich-girl act if I hadn't had Mo and Flo's house to use. Maybe I could have, but driving up to the brick mansion and seeing the gigantic metal *V* woven into the locked wrought-iron gate sure softened up old Brother Perfect Robert. He was thinking *V* for Vanderbelt. I was thinking it was a good thing that many rich people left their names off their mailboxes. I had him stop the Lincoln in front of the gate. I got out.

"Don't you want a ride to the door?"

"No thank you," I said. I rang the buzzer in the gate, then stood there trying to look bored. Actually I was holding my breath. If George, the butler, was not home, my plan would be ruined. A rich orphan kid like me would naturally have a way to get into her own house if nobody was around to open the gate—other than climbing a six-foot-high iron fence. A voice came over the intercom on the gate.

"Yes? Who is it?" Now this was the trickiest moment of all. I couldn't very well say "Sherelee" and ruin the Vanderbelt story. I crossed my fingers and said, "Hi, George, it's me." Again, luck played a part in my plan. George not only recognized my voice, but he did not say anything to suggest I was not the young mistress of the house. The buzzer sounded, and the gate popped open. I slipped in and slammed it behind me.

"See you, I guess," I said to BP Robert. "Thanks for the meal and the ride." By this time, George was holding open the front door of the house. I turned my back on BP Robert and walked to the house. I heard him start the car knowing that the last thing he would see as he drove away from the big house was Mo and Flo's yacht tied to the dock at the bottom of the lawn.

"Ho, little con queen! What's up?" asked George.

"I can't tell you. I'm on a case."

"Hey. All reet. You probably used your noggin to do some tall headwork. Last I heard, you were going to bend your brain and fill your head with higher ed. before you trod the path of famous tailettes. What gives?"

35

"Something came up."

"Ah," said George. "How about some cool cow juice and some cooler chatologue?"

In the kitchen, George sat with me, and we drank glasses of ice cold milk. It was the first recognizable nutrition I had received all day.

"You know, little gumshoe, I always have thought your granddad Sherlock was the bossest dude around. He was real heavy on the gray matter—had a real savvy conk—a highbrow dude who hit on all cylinders at all times. Except when he was stuffing dopium up his nose or harpooning the gunk into his arms—but if he were perfect, he wouldn't be real—right?"

"Right."

"For a sec, I was bummed out that such a small dolly such as yourself should embark on a tough career at so tender an age. But I'm mellow now, mama. If you find yourself in a bind —for instance, maybe if you have to cop a lam and need a lift —just call. You're OK, little Holmes. You're one swell dudette."

George is possibly the greatest human being I know. I love listening to him talk. Usually I figure out most of what he is saying—usually. Flo and Mo have made a lifetime project of listing all the slang words George knows. Each time they think they've got them all, George comes up with more— some a hundred years old.

After we finished the milk, I told George everything. He thought my plan was brilliant and—as he put it—I was one smart skirt.

Of Myra he said that he couldn't see how such a boneheaded saphead—such a rattle-beaned, hen-headed, featherminded twit—could be my older sister. He also added that he liked Myra and hoped she would outgrow it. George is a kindly person. He is also an optimist.

George drove me home. His last words to me that day were, "Call on me, fly moll. And don't worry, I won't blow your cover. Now I'll do a scram."

I stood at the curb and watched eighty-two-year-old George grind the gears of the Vogel limousine as he peeled away from our house. The screaming tires left lots of rubber on the road. As I walked up the path, admiring George's style, I thought that maybe I should fire Joan Watson.

# 12

It was pretty late when I got home. My mother was in the kitchen preparing dinner. When she heard the door slam, she called, "Myra, come in here and set the table."

I hollered back, "It's Sherelee, Mom. Myra's not here." I didn't feel like explaining reality to her just yet.

I was not to be spared. "Then you come in here and do it. I'm running behind schedule."

"Hi, Mom." I tried to sound cheerful.

"Where have you been all afternoon, Sherelee? Joan Watkins called hours ago looking for you. Didn't your father ground you? I'm sure he will have something to say to you tonight after dinner."

Watson was an award-winning dud. All she had to do was avoid running into my family while I was out detecting, and she went and telephoned my house. If Watson hadn't called my mother's attention to my absence, it probably would not have been noticed. Well, sometimes the truth is the best defense. "I was over at Flo and Mo's visiting with George."

"At least you weren't at the mall or wandering around downtown. How did you get home?"

A smart detective knows that the whole truth is not always necessary. The time to lie a little had arrived. "I took a bus —that's why I was so late."

"That's good. You know how I hate for you to ride with George. They should take his license away because he's a madman on the road. I don't see why Flo doesn't just give him a pension and send him to Florida. The Vogels certainly can afford it."

"George doesn't want to retire, and he hates hot weather. Besides, whenever they go anyplace, George sits in the back with Flo, and Mo does the driving. Mo likes to drive the limousine. He especially likes wearing the chauffeur cap."

"Strange people—the bunch of them. Have you seen your sister around?"

I was still not ready to say anything about Myra. I figured that it would be better to break the news when my father was home. I had run out of cheerful small talk. I had finished setting the table—the four usual places to avoid more questions—so I announced, "I have to go do homework now. See you at dinner."

"Thank you, Sherelee. I'll have your sister clear the table tonight. You shouldn't be required to do both jobs. By the way, you haven't answered my question. Have you seen her?"

"No, Mom."

"Well, she'll be here for dinner, and I'll have a talk with her about responsibility. She's supposed to set an example for you —not the other way around."

I almost ran to my room. I figured I would have enough time before dinner to read the Temple of Perfection pamphlets. I wanted to know as much as possible before chaos took over.

As it turned out, there was more than enough time. The pamphlets, entitled *Spiritual Perfection Through a Perfect Teacher I* and *II,* were too boring to read. I skimmed over the

38

parts about the good works performed by the Temple of Perfection—all of which seemed really dinky and inexpensive. For example, the Temple served soup to twenty poor people one Christmas. Either the Temple of Perfection was very broke or very cheap.

There was a list of elaborate plans called Perfectly Planned Perfect Philanthropic Projects for the Future in the second pamphlet. It included a leper colony and a tuberculosis sanatorium for the poor. As far as I know, both of those projects are completely unnecessary in today's world of modern medicine.

My favorite Perfect Project for the Future was a four-lane highway, condominium and shopping-center complex for Central Borneo. The footnote explaining the perfectness of this plan was smudged. Underneath the list of projects was a dotted line. Under the dotted line was a contribution form one could fill out.

Both pamphlets were illustrated with lots of photos of Daddy Perfect—unsmiling—and snapshots of Temple of Perfection members—grinning real face-breaker grins. The boring text didn't seem to say anything about what the Temple of Perfection taught or what its members believed in. It did say a whole lot—over and over again—about how turning your life over to the TOP would bring you eternal happiness and perfection. The word *love* appeared in every other sentence—most of the time with the word *perfect* before it.

I wondered what exactly about the Temple of Perfection had grabbed Myra's attention enough to get her to join. I was sure she had never read the dull pamphlets. The clue must be with the recruiters. A rescue plan began to take shape in my head. I was interrupted by my father's voice.

"Come in to dinner, girls."

This was it. The awful moment of truth. There are times when it cannot be avoided.

I sat down at the table. "Go get your sister, Sherelee. The casserole will get cold." My mother was spooning great globs of whitish stuff onto plates.

I didn't move. "She's not coming to dinner," I said.

"What do you mean? Go tell her we want her here."

"I can't." My mother stopped dishing out the mystery contents of the casserole and stared at me.

"You're giving me trouble again, aren't you, Sherelee? I said for you to go get your sister."

"I can't. I'm trying to tell you. I tried to tell you yesterday, but you wouldn't listen. She's gone. She's flown the coop, taken a powder, busted out, done a cold sneak, done a scram, gone on the lam. . . ." I was really getting revved up. I hadn't realized how much of George's slang I could remember. I had been so tense that I felt as if I were unwinding like a giant talking toy. I couldn't stop myself. ". . . done a dust, a fade, a heel and toe . . ."

My father helped me. He stuck his face close to mine and said menacingly, "Shut up, Sherelee, this second." It worked. I suddenly couldn't remember any more slang.

"Stop being fresh to your mother. And why are you talking like that? Have you been hanging around with George again? Do as your mother says—go get your sister. That's an order!"

I couldn't take any more. It is one thing living with a mush-headed family in ordinary times, but in a time of crisis, it is infuriating. I lifted my now-filled plate off the table, turned it upside down and mashed the contents into the table-cloth. Then I got up from my seat and ran to my room. Naturally they followed me.

Both parents burst into the room together. I sat calmly on my bed, pointing. They followed the direction of my point. It took them a minute to register what they were seeing, but it finally got to their brains.

"Oh my Lord," said my mother, "where are Myra's things?"

40

"Where is Myra?" said my father.

"Myra, MYRA," my mother called as she pulled open the closet door and saw that Myra's clothing was gone. She rushed over to the dresser and pulled open empty drawers. All the while she was calling, "Myra, Myra, Myra." Her voice got louder and louder.

"It's true," my father mumbled. "It's true."

My mother was getting hysterical. She was down on her knees looking under Myra's bed; she was up, pulling open Myra's desk drawer. Then, finally, she stood in the middle of the room, tears streaming down her face, calling Myra's name.

My father walked over to her and shook her—hard. My mother stopped wailing. Then he turned to me. "What have you been trying to tell us, Sherelee?"

I told them about noticing Myra's things disappearing. I told them about how I followed her to the thrift store. I told them about seeing her get into a big van and drive away. I did not tell them about my plan to rescue her. I am compassionate, but I am not a fool.

Suddenly my mother, who had been standing in one spot silently weeping, came to life. "The police!" she screamed. "We must call the police. Myra is a minor. It's kidnapping."

"Yes, of course, dear," said my father. He put his arm around my mother and led her back to the kitchen. He dialed the police. After a few minutes, he hung up the phone. "Let's finish our dinner. A detective will be here in about half an hour."

"How can you eat at a time like this? Sherelee, clean up the table, please."

"I'm hungry," said my father. "I had a long, hard day at work. I can't think straight on an empty stomach."

"Me neither," I added. My mother looked disgusted. She threw the contents of her own plate into the garbage. I put the casserole in the microwave and got myself a clean plate. My father and I ate the unidentifiable food in silence. It was almost as bad as it looked. With my mother's absence from the table, both my father and I felt free to use a liberal amount of catsup.

As I swallowed my first mouthful of catsup-coated glop, I thought I could hear my brain cells screaming at me—"Not MORE sugar! Feed us steak!"

# 13

I was standing on the porch when the police car pulled up. I was excited about observing a modern-day police detective in action.

"This the Holmes house, girlie?" asked the large, squarish man sporting a flat crewcut and wearing a plaid jacket.

"Yes, sir," I said in my most respectful voice. I opened the front door.

What happened during the next forty-five minutes was not at all what I expected.

"Now what's this about a kidnapping? Who's missing? Have you gotten a ransom note or phone call yet?" The plainclothes policeman pulled out a little notepad and clicked his ballpoint pen. "My name is Detective Abbott. Just give me the facts," he announced.

At first there was a great deal of confusion about police terminology. It took a half hour for Detective Abbott to get my parents to understand why the police did not use the words *kidnapping* or *abduction* when referring to kids who ran away from home. This was particularly true when the runaway was observed both leaving home and voluntarily joining members of a cult.

When Detective Abbott finally announced that from all he

had heard, Myra was not a kidnap victim but a runaway and that the police did not have the manpower to look for every kid who ran away from home, my mother collapsed. My father called the doctor. Detective Abbott crumbled the pages he had been writing on, stuffed them into his pocket, apologized and stood up to leave.

Just before he stepped outside, he said, "Of course, you could swear out a warrant for your daughter's arrest since she did steal things from this house. Then maybe we could pick her up—if we could find her, of course." Fortunately, nobody but me heard him.

"Thank you," I said and quickly closed the door. I made myself scarce. The doctor would come and probably sedate my mom—and maybe my dad, too. I had important work to do. I went into the garage.

My mother saves newspapers—and magazines and pamphlets and any other kind of disposable literature she gets her hands on. She stacks everything neatly against the back wall of the garage.

When I entered the garage that evening, it was near the end of a two-year collection period. Our car hadn't been under its own roof for six months. I walked around the piles of written material and wondered if I could possibly find what I was looking for.

Fortunately, my mother is a very orderly saver of paper. She stacks newspapers and magazines by date and by publication. I discovered that each pile of newspapers contained exactly two months' worth of daily papers. This made my task easier because I was only interested in special issues of our local paper, the *Daily Truth*. It isn't a very thick newspaper or, many complain, a very interesting one, but it's our only local paper. People buy it mostly for announcements of births, weddings, funerals, garage sales, store sales and to line the bottom of their bird cages.

Just once, the editor hired a young reporter who actually

managed to find some news to write about. She wrote a detailed, exciting, investigative report that ran a full week, took up much of the space in the newspaper and won her a Pulitzer prize. The same week the prize was announced, she was hired away by a large newspaper in New York City. The series of articles was about the Temple of Perfection.

I remembered them because for months after their publication, wherever you went in town, you heard people arguing about the Temple of Perfection, cults in general, dangers to modern youth and the good old days when things were safe. As soon as the ace reporter left town, the *Daily Truth* immediately returned to being its old, boring self, and all interest in cult matters seemed to fade away.

It didn't take long for me to find the issues I needed. I pulled them from their pile and went to my room. The police might not have the manpower to find Myra—but manpower wasn't what was needed. This was a job for a single, keen, detecting mind—mine.

# 14

I had just finished reading the first article about the Temple of Perfection. It contained a detailed description of TOP headquarters, the home of Daddy Perfect and his family and the place where new recruits were taken to be indoctrinated.

The article not only gave the exact location of the headquarters, but described the buildings, the grounds and the methods used to protect them. There was even a map showing the entire twenty-acre compound. It included the security posts, the electric fences and the gates.

What a job of detecting that ace reporter had done! I was

reaching for the second article when my father called me. I looked at my watch; it was ten o'clock. I had been awake for sixteen hours.

There was a strange woman standing in the middle of our living room. When I say *strange,* I mean a stranger to me as well as strange-looking.

"Sherelee, this is your Aunt Irene Holmes," my father said, yawning. "The doctor has given both your mother and me pills to help us sleep tonight. Irene will be in charge of things around here until your mother has recovered from the shock a bit. Please don't give her any trouble. Good night."

Without further explanation, my father gave me a kiss and exited. I stared at Irene Holmes. She hadn't moved at all. In fact, she hadn't even blinked an eye. She stared at me. I was dumbfounded.

I had heard stories about Irene Holmes—my father's youngest sister—my entire life. Over the years, she had sent us postcards from places like Tibet and Nepal and China. But I had actually met Irene only once—when I was two years old. My mother had always refused to discuss Irene except to say that she was irresponsible. Whenever a postcard would arrive, my father would get a dreamy look on his face. Then for days he would walk around smiling and talking about what an unusual person his baby sister had turned into and what an exciting life she led.

My mother, on the other hand, always referred to Irene as a hippie. My father called her an adventurer. I once asked how Irene could afford to travel endlessly, since, as far as I knew, none of the Holmeses had inherited a fortune.

It was then that I heard the story of my Aunt Irene's first great adventure. My father told me that the day she graduated from college, Irene slipped a note into my father's pocket, handed him her cap and gown and excused herself. She was not seen again for a year. At her graduation dinner, attended by all the Holmeses except Irene, my father read the note to the gathering.

It said:

> Dear family,
> I have gone to seek adventure and fortune.
> Don't worry. Have a nice party.
>
> > Love,
> > Irene

It was the first and last time every single Holmes shared the same opinion. From the youngest to the oldest, they were ticked off at Irene. Several suggested that she be disowned. There was a whole lot of shouting and arm waving. Finally, my grandmother told them all to shut up and eat before their dinners got cold.

My father said that feelings cooled down after a few months. When Irene returned, she was rich. Irene gave an elegant dinner at a fancy hotel for the whole family. After dessert, Irene stood up and made a speech. She apologized for her abrupt departure but said it had been necessary. Irene refused to provide the family with details of her discovery but told the gathered Holmes clan that she had found the legendary lost treasure of the famous pirate and privateer Captain Kidd.

She explained that instead of hanging around drinking beer in college, she had spent all of her spare time in various libraries researching lost treasures. Early on, Irene had decided that sunken ships didn't interest her. She wanted the challenge of finding what someone who was diabolically clever had deliberately hidden. In particular, she wanted to find Captain Kidd's treasure—a hoard of gold and jewels sought after by thousands and never found.

Irene explained to the family that it took a Holmes mind to find something that had eluded the rest of mankind for

46

almost three hundred years. Irene finished and sat down. She expected praise. She expected congratulations. She expected her family to share her happiness.

Instead she got disbelief. She got skepticism. She even got a few boos and jeers. Most of the Holmeses thought Irene was pulling their legs. Some even doubted if she was rich. Others accused her of making her money in various illegal ways. One cousin said she was sure Irene had simply gone and married a millionaire. My father was the only Holmes to believe her. He stood up and said so. He got jeered and booed. Irene left the table, left the room and, a few days later, left the country. As far as I knew, she had only returned once—when I was two.

Apparently her purpose was to borrow me for a few years. My mother, who had never met Irene before, naturally said no.

Now she stood facing me in the living room of my own house—a large-nosed, tall, thin, muscular woman wearing a high-collared, ankle-length tweed coat, which had a short cape attached to it. On her head was a matching hat—with peaks both front and back. Irene Holmes was wearing the exact outfit worn by my Great-great-grandfather Sherlock when he went detecting.

"Your mouth is open. Do you wish to say something?" Irene spoke as she removed her cape-coat.

"Uhhh," was all I could manage. Underneath her coat, Irene was wearing a safari shirt and baggy paratrooper pants tucked into calf-high, tightly laced army boots.

"If I remember correctly, the kitchen is this way. Come with me, Sherelee." Irene tossed her coat and hat onto the sofa and headed for the kitchen. I followed.

# 15

"Speak!" Irene and I were sitting at the kitchen table drinking orange juice. I had not been able to say a single word. Irene refilled my glass.

"I realize I am something of a shock to you, Niece. I also realize that you have been awake far too many hours for you to function efficiently. However, you have a case to solve, and I have come a very long way to assist you."

"How long a way?" My voice was finally working.

"Very long. Tibet," answered Irene.

"Tibet?" I said. "That's impossible. Myra only disappeared this morning."

"Good. Good. I always knew you would take up the Holmes mantle and wear it into the battle against crime and deception." Irene was smiling at me. It felt really good to be praised by Irene, a family member who understood our important place in history.

"How come you are here, Aunt Irene?"

"I-REE-NEE, Sherelee. I prefer the Antique pronunciation of my name—and please drop the *Aunt.*"

"OK. What about Tibet?"

"Well, I have come from Tibet—but not directly. I have been traveling for three weeks. Myra's disappearance is simply a coincidence. I was intending to visit some of my relatives and offer my forgiveness to them. I was also intending to petition your mother and father once again."

"Do you still want to take me with you?" I blurted. I felt a chill of excitement go up my back.

"Ah, they've told you. Certainly. I never change my mind about important things. But let us set that aside for now.

48

Tell me how you have approached this problem of Myra."

"Me, Irene? What makes you think I've approached it at all?"

"I am a Holmes, am I not? I am, in fact, one generation closer to Sherlock than you, am I not? Do you not believe that I possess infinitely fine powers of observation, reasoning and deduction? Is it not completely logical that you, Sherelee Holmes, should continue the line of great thinkers and enemies of crime? Is it not obvious that you would find the disappearance of your sister irresistible? Did not your father tell me that you have been out, following Myra?"

"Yes, I mean no . . . yes. That's too many questions at once. You're right. I have a plan."

Irene leaned her chair against the refrigerator and put her feet up on the kitchen table. "Tell me all, Niece."

I told her everything. By the time I was finished talking, it was almost one o'clock in the morning.

"Brilliant, Niece. You may turn out to be the greatest Holmes of all. I offer my assistance to you—I am not without resources and certain expertise which may come in handy. Do you accept?"

"Yes, Irene. Thank you."

"Good. Now go to bed. Sleep in. I will meet you here at eight o'clock sharp. I shall prepare a hearty breakfast for us."

Irene patted me on the back and pushed me toward the door. I stumbled to my bedroom and fell asleep without taking off my clothes. The last thing I remember thinking was that two remarkable people had offered to help me—George and Irene. Myra was as good as home—this case would be a breeze.

"Why aren't you eating your food, Sherelee? You must have nourishment or your brain won't work to capacity."

It was eight thirty, and I couldn't seem to wake up completely. Irene had dragged me out of bed at eight o'clock.

Even after taking a cold shower and getting dressed, I was half-asleep. The food sitting in the dishes in front of me was not helping the situation.

"What is this stuff, Irene?"

"Stuff? STUFF? You have never seen kippered herrings before—one of your great-great-grandfather's favorite breakfast treats? And that aromatic cereal is tsampa, a Tibetan staple. I wouldn't go anywhere in the world without the ingredients necessary to create it. Eat. Drink. Expand your horizons!"

I picked up the bowl with the tsampa in it. "It smells rancid, Irene. Maybe it spoiled while you were traveling."

"Acute observation! It IS rancid. Tsampa is a mixture made primarily from barley and rancid yak butter. Eat. Enjoy."

"I'll throw up if I have to eat the tsampa—and I can't eat those bony, ugly, smelly, dried-out fish either. I'm sorry, Irene."

"Don't be sorry, Sherelee. You simply lack an adventurer's palate. It is something you will someday acquire. May I scramble you some eggs and toast you some toast? I think I remember how to cook our simple native food."

Irene got me to drink a cup of special herb tea. It didn't taste great, but it woke me right up.

At nine o'clock, I telephoned Watson. "Watson, listen carefully. I desperately need your help again." Watson interrupted me with a groan. I ignored it.

"This is a big mission, Watson, but we're not in it alone."

"Awwwww, Sherelee, why don't we just go to a movie?"

I was getting angry. "Watson, you bimbo, this is for real. Myra has run away to the Temple of Perfection. She's probably out at their headquarters and couldn't escape if she wanted to. So cut out the whining and tell me—are you going to help or not? Make up your mind. NOW!"

I was especially firm because I was on a tight schedule. I

didn't have an hour to waste convincing Watson. I could have dumped her as an assistant, but it is not a good idea to begin a precise plan by changing it.

"REALLY? Myra really took off with a cult? Wow. Don't those Temple people wear funny outfits and shave their heads?" Watson started giggling.

"No, Watson. You have your cults mixed up. And stop laughing. It's not funny. How would you feel if Arnold, your supposedly terrific brother, ran away to a cult? How would you feel if you got lured away and nobody came to rescue you?" Watson stopped laughing.

"Arnold would never do that, Sherelee. He'd never miss football practice. And I'd be afraid to leave home. . . ."

"WATSON, YOU MAKE ME CRAZY," I shouted. "Are you going to help me or not?"

"Sure. What are friends for? What do I have to do, Sherelee?"

"Pack an overnight bag. Bring your bathing suit, tennis stuff and pajamas. Get permission to stay at the Vogel house with me. Tell your mom my Aunt Irene is going to stay with us."

"Pack an overnight bag . . . ?"

"Don't repeat everything, Watson. Just do it." I hung up on her.

I turned to Irene. "Would you tell my dad that you are taking me and Watson to the Vogels for the weekend to distract me and to keep me out of his way?"

"Certainly, Niece. It would be my pleasure." The phone rang as I was thinking how nice it was having an assistant who didn't question every small detail.

"This is Mrs. Watkins, Sherelee. What's this about going to the Vogel house? Let me speak to your mother."

I put the phone down and ran to get Irene. A good detective must always be ready to think on her feet and make minor adjustments to suit the situation. This was one such time. As I knew she would, Irene did a masterful snow job on Watson's mother. At the end of ten minutes, they were laughing and chatting like old friends. Watson's mother gave permission for Watson to stay away not one but two nights.

Confident that events were moving in the right direction, I packed my own suitcase.

# 16

"Stop whimpering, Watson!" I whispered.

Watson was curled up on the backseat of Irene's old Volvo. I was sitting on the floor between the back and front seats, covered with a blanket. It was essential that my relationship to Irene be hidden from the Temple of Perfection people. The last thing I wanted was to be spotted riding around in a ratty, old, rattletrap of a car.

"How old is this car, Irene?" I asked, thinking that casual conversation would calm Watson.

"Only twenty years old—remarkable machine, isn't it? It's never been garaged a day in its life."

I could see the ground rushing by underneath my knee, where a piece of the floor had rusted away. "It sure is, Irene."

"Watson, why are you making those strange noises? Are you in pain?" Irene spoke over her shoulder while she guided the disintegrating car into traffic.

"My name is Watkins, Miss Holmes—Joan Watkins—and I'm scared. Where are we going? Why are we downtown? This isn't the way to the Vogels' house. Why is Sherelee hiding on the floor?" Watson spoke in her usual whine.

"You really must learn to modulate your voice, Watson.

Perhaps training by a good voice teacher might help you. And it is Ms. Holmes, Holmes or Irene—I-REE-NEE."

"And please call me Watkins or Joan, Irene."

"Why?" asked Irene. I liked my aunt better every minute.

"Because those are my real names, Irene."

"Nonsense. Every Holmes needs a Watson when conducting an investigation. For the lack of any other candidates, you are it."

Watson squeaked—like an enormous mouse.

Irene jammed on the brakes and pulled the car off the road. She turned in her seat, reached out and grabbed Watson's hand. I slid the blanket away from my face and watched.

Irene did not speak. She stared into Watson's eyes. Watson sat up slowly. Her normally tense shoulders relaxed. Her pinched, nervous face relaxed. She didn't look afraid. Irene released Watson's hand and turned to restart the car. Watson leaned back against the seat looking happy.

"What did you do to her, Irene?" I asked.

"Just a little Tibetan trick. It won't last more than an hour or so, but by then we'll all be out of this vehicle. Now get ready, we're almost there."

I untangled myself from the blanket while Irene backed the car into the alleyway next to the UFO Bookstore and Information Exchange. Using the open door to shield me from passersby on the street, I slid out of the car and knocked on the delivery door.

"Bring the cigars?" rasped a voice as the door flew open.

"Don't I always?" I answered and rushed past him into the chaos of the store. I kept the box of Marsh Wheelings tightly clamped under my arm.

"Give and you get," said Harry, the proprietor of the messiest store in town.

I had discovered the UFO Bookstore and Information Exchange the year before. It was possibly the most interesting place in town. In addition to the thousands of books which were stacked against the walls and in the aisles, spilling off shelves and crammed into cartons, there was Harry. Harry called himself an information broker. He usually sat in an old easy chair near the front door, drinking coffee and smoking cigars and waiting for customers.

Harry refused to have any kind of conversation with anyone unless he was paid. This included information about where a certain book might be located. Despite the fact that books were shoved anywhere at random when they came into the store, Harry could locate any title in a matter of minutes. Since it could take a customer hours or even days to find a particular book in the mess, it was worthwhile to pay Harry to do it for you.

Harry did not accept money for information. He only accepted Marsh Wheeling cigars—the number of cigars depending upon Harry's mood and the bargaining ability of the seeker. Information was usually more expensive than book finding because Harry made a profit on the sale of each book.

When dealing with Harry, you had to avoid telling him any secret because he had no qualms about selling it to the next customer who walked in. That day, I chose my words carefully.

"Harry, today I need information."

"Give and you get." Harry held out his hand.

"How much, Harry?"

"What's the subject?"

"The Temple of Perfection."

"Ahhh, cult information. Twelve Marsh Wheelings."

"Three, Harry."

"Ten."

"Four, Harry, and all I'll ask is one question."

"Seven, and I'll come up with something special."

"Five if you have the information."

"I always have the information."

"If someone wanted to leave the Temple of Perfection compound without being seen, how would she do it?"

"Hah! You want a million-dollar answer, and I sold out to you for five cigars. But a bargain is a bargain. The tunnel."

"That's it—the tunnel? There's a tunnel there?"

"Wouldn't have said so if there wasn't."

"Where is it and where does it go?"

"Two more cigars."

"One more, Harry."

"You are a hard bargainer, kid. OK. I'm feeling kind today. Besides, I hate to admit that even Harry doesn't know where the tunnel starts, but it lets out on old Route 1. Now give."

I handed the cigar box over to Harry. There was no need to open it because six cigars was all I had. Harry lifted the lid and nodded. I reminded myself to note the cigars as a major expense of this case.

"Thanks, Harry." I made my way to the door.

"No sweat. Why do you want that information anyway? You can tell old Harry."

"I'm writing a paper for school." I lied. Harry looked disappointed.

"Get what you needed, Niece?" Irene backed the car out of the alley.

"Sort of. It will help."

"Good work, old girl."

Nothing else was said until we reached the Vogel mansion.

# 17

"George, do you have something to report?" I asked.

"You bet, little moll. We're closing in on the bosseteer. He had his flunky, bad baby, pug-ugly mug give me a buzz on the old hellophone at the gate. The bimblestiff was giving us the I-see, trying to shepherd the little bloodhound." George stopped to take a breath.

I had been watching Irene while George spoke. She was nodding her head and smiling. Naturally a Holmes of her experience would understand George. On the other hand, Watson looked confused.

George continued. "Well, the babbling brook wanted to gab with our baby big eyes, but I alibied the little sneaker and put her at a sit-down with her mouthpiece—just like you said to, sweet baby lady." George smiled at me.

Watson sighed. "I don't understand any of this, Sherelee. What is George saying?"

"George just explained that he feels we are closing in on Daddy Perfect—the bosseteer, or big cheese. What that means is that the Temple of Perfection people are seriously interested in us or, rather, me—events are following my carefully worked-out plan. Things are going well, Watson."

Watson began a low moan, then cut it off by clamping her hand over her own mouth. I was amazed. Irene winked at me. I continued translating George's report.

"George also said that this underling of Daddy Perfect telephoned from the gate. He wanted to speak to me—in my guise of Cynthia Vanderbelt."

"Cynthia who? Who is Cynthia?" Watson interrupted.

I ignored her and went on. "George figured that the lowlife was spying on Cynthia—checking up on her identity to make sure she is for real. George told him that Cynthia was at a meeting with her lawyers."

"Who is Cynthia?" The whine was creeping back into Watson's voice.

"I'M Cynthia. It's my disguise. Now let's get organized."

"I still don't understand any of this."

56

"There'll be plenty of time for explaining later, Watson. Let's just get to work.

"This kitchen will be our command post. There will have to be one of you here twenty-four hours around the clock until phase four of my plan is completed, and Myra is rescued. You are my backup crew."

I walked over to the kitchen wall phone and dialed the Nearly Perfect Shoppe. A man answered.

"Yes?" He sounded angry.

"May I please speak to BP Robert? This is—" The man cut me off.

"Why aren't you working? You can speak to him tonight after evening meal. Whatever petty business you have can wait. I'm trying to keep this line free." He hung up.

I dialed again. Obviously the man had mistaken me for a cult member.

"Yes?"

I had deduced why he was keeping the line free and changed my approach accordingly. "This is Cynthia Vanderbelt. May I please talk to BP Robert?"

"Cynthia Vanderbelt? How nice to get to speak to you. Brother Robert is not here just now. I am BP Lawton, First Class. May I help you?" BP Lawton, First Class, suddenly sounded as if he had drunk a quart of maple syrup.

"First Class?" I asked.

"Oh, that's just a little title bestowed upon me by our Beloved Daddy Perfect. You may call me Brother Lawton or BP Lawton if you prefer."

"Thanks," I said. "I'll just leave a message for BP Robert. Tell him I was going to stop by to talk to him. It's sort of an emergency. I'll try to reach him later—or tomorrow. Good-bye. . . ."

"WAIT!" BP Lawton shouted. "Maybe I can help you. Why don't you come down to the shop and talk to me?"

57

"Well, I don't know. It's about my joining the Temple of Perfection. Do you know how I could go about doing that?"

I could hear the man take a deep breath to calm himself. "Certainly, Little Sister. Certainly."

"Well, then, maybe I'll go over to the shop later this morning."

"Do you need a lift, Little Sister? How would you like a ride in a shiny new Rolls-Royce?"

"No, thank you. My chauffeur will drive me over there." I hung up the phone.

"All goes well, Niece?" Irene asked.

"All goes well, Irene," I answered. "Let's get going, George. I'll be in touch when I can get to a phone."

"What's happening here, Sherelee? I thought we were going to hang out and swim and play tennis this weekend. Where are you going?"

"Undercover, Watson. Undercover."

The last thing I heard as I got into the backseat of the limousine was a loud wailing sound coming from the kitchen.

I didn't speak to George once we were out of the driveway. I meditated and worked on getting into character. By the time we reached the Nearly Perfect Shoppe, I was Cynthia Vanderbelt, spoiled, rich, bored brat. George opened the door of the limo for me and tipped his hat. I hoped I would see him again soon. Every detective is aware of the danger of going into the heart of the enemy's camp. I didn't have much time to think about it, because several people rushed from the store and practically carried me inside.

I was able to turn my head and see George steer the car into traffic in the most dignified manner. He, too, was playing his part well.

I looked at the smiling adults surrounding me. I smiled back at them. I was on my own.

# 18

When I entered the Nearly Perfect Shoppe as Cynthia Vanderbelt, millionaire child, I called all of my Holmes talents into play. I was prepared for anything. I was expecting to be grilled, cross-examined and brainwashed. I was ready to resist inwardly while giving in outwardly. Cynthia would join the Temple of Perfection. Sherelee would remain detached—observing and detecting.

I was sure the next few hours would be the most challenging in my life. I was wrong. They were the most boring. At first, I thought it was some kind of cult trick—lull the unsuspecting kid into a stupor and then grab her. But after a short while, I realized that nothing exciting was going to happen. I was disappointed that I had spent my energy forcing myself to stay alert.

We sipped herb tea. We munched on rock-hard little cookies. Brother Perfect Lawton, First Class, did most of the talking. Everyone smiled all of the time. I kept a sullen pout on my face—it seemed to make them try harder, in their dull way.

I was told that joining the Temple of Perfection would mean I would be among the Very Few Truly Blessed in this world—because I would be following Daddy Perfect up the Golden Path into the Perfect Peace of the Everlasting Glory of Heaven. That's how they spoke—and they went on for hours.

When they were through telling me all the wonderful things about the Temple of Perfection, BP Lawton, First Class, went into the kitchen and returned with a big piece of chocolate cake, which he set down in front of me.

"Now let us talk about you, you poor child. Unburden yourself, Little Sister. Join our Temple. Find Perfect Happiness. Tell us your troubles. Tell us about your meeting with the lawyers."

During the several hours of droning talk about the Temple, BP Lawton had explained that there was a three-month probation period during which time candidates could make up their minds while doing services for the Temple—like bringing love gifts to the Nearly Perfect Shoppe. My research had revealed that there were Temple outposts in five other cities. Putting the facts together, I concluded that I didn't have three months to wait around. Myra could be long gone in that time—shipped out of town to work in one of the outposts.

The moment had come for my big performance. This was the trickiest and weakest part of my plan.

I got up and pretended to head for the door.

"Where are you going?" asked a Sister Perfect, Premium Grade—the one called Ramona.

"Well, I am interested in joining you, but I don't have time to wait three months—or one month or even a week. So good-bye."

"What do you mean?" asked BP Lawton.

"My lawyers are planning to get a court order to send me out of the country until I am eighteen," I lied.

"Is that possible?" asked the other Brother Perfect.

"Anything is possible with lawyers," I answered.

"Why would they do that to you?" The Sisters and Brothers looked nervous. They were about to lose the Vanderbelt millions.

"Because my parents, although very wealthy, were free spirits. They believed that money wasn't really important. In their will, they gave me full control of the Vanderbelt assets —on my fifteenth birthday." I stopped to take a sip of tea. The four adults were sitting on the edges of their chairs, mouths hanging open.

"How wealthy were your parents?" blurted the Brother Perfect, Premium Grade.

BP Lawton glared at him. "Shhh. Let the child tell her story. Go on, Cynthia. Unburden yourself further."

"OK. Fifteen," I said and paused again.

"Fifteen? Fifteen what?" asked BP Lawton.

"Fifteen million dollars. That's how wealthy my parents were. That's what the estate is worth, more or less."

The cult members had all picked up their cups and were busily sipping tea. At least two of them looked a little pale—like they might faint. "Do you really want to hear the rest of my story? You must be bored with it," I said wistfully.

"Of course we want to hear you tell your sad tale. Please continue. No one else will interrupt you." There was a hard edge in BP Lawton's voice. For the first time, people stopped smiling—but just for a minute or so.

"I am now fourteen," I lied further. "My lawyers think that the will is irresponsible—especially since they now control the estate. They want me safely out of the way for a few years so I can't get my hands on the money. You see, the only restriction in the will was that I be in the United States on my fifteenth birthday to assume responsibility. If I am out of the country, I have to live on an allowance until I am eighteen."

As I listened to myself, I realized what a ridiculous story I had concocted. It wasn't that I didn't look like a person about to be fifteen—kids mature at different paces—but the story was so dumb. I was ready for them to begin chopping it to pieces. I wished I had had more time to think things through.

There was a full minute of silence. During it, I walked slowly toward the door of the shop. I couldn't let my own doubts destroy my plan. I was a dejected Cynthia Vanderbelt walking out into the world, away from what they had called the Perfect Family.

"Stop! Wait! Don't go." It was Brother Perfect Lawton, First Class.

I turned to face him. I had managed to squeeze about four tears from my eyes.

"Why? I might as well go home and pack. By tomorrow night, I'll be on a plane to Switzerland—boarding school, you know."

"No," said BP Lawton. "Not if you don't want to. Are you really interested in joining the Temple of Perfection Perfect Family?"

"Yes," I answered.

"Just give me a minute to make a phone call."

BP Lawton came back to our little group, beaming. "You're in, Little Sister, you're in. Daddy Perfect has given his permission to waive the usual Time of Testing candidates must go through. Because of your extreme need at the moment, our Perfect Parents, Daddy and Mommy Perfect, want to adopt you immediately."

"Adopt me? I don't want to be adopted," I said.

"I was speaking spiritually, of course. The Perfects have decided that, as of this moment, you are a member of our Blessed Temple of Perfection Family. Welcome, Little Sister."

"But what about the love gifts you told me about? What about proving my sincerity?" I protested weakly as the Perfect Sisters hugged me.

"Daddy Perfect said that in your case, love gifts and tests of sincerity are not necessary. Daddy Perfect knows all. He sees deep into the spirit of each of us. He said you are ready to join us. However, if there is anything you want to get from your home to bring with you . . ." BP Lawton looked hopeful.

"If I go home, there will probably be a lawyer or two

62

waiting for me. They'll never let me go to the Garden of Perfection with you."

"Then let's just be off."

I was rushed out of the shop and into the backseat of a Rolls-Royce. I settled against the soft leather seat between the two Sisters Perfect and thought about how Myra had made her first trip to the Garden of Perfection in the back of a rattling van.

As we drove off, I thought I spotted Irene lurking across the street. On the way to the Garden of Perfection, I managed to look out the back window. In the distance, I could see a dark speck of a car. Thinking that it might be Irene's Volvo following us made me feel secure. Everything was going exactly as I had planned.

The good feeling lasted until the electrified gates of the Garden of Perfection slammed closed behind us.

# 19

"This," announced the Premium Grade Brother, "is the Garden of Perfection, the Hallowed Home of Daddy Perfect."

"And, from now on, Little Sister, your home, too," added the Sister on my right.

About twenty smiling people in light blue jumpsuits were mowing lawns, pulling weeds, watering plants, sweeping paths, carrying big garbage bags—there wasn't a scrap of paper or a fallen leaf or broken twig anywhere in sight.

"Get out!" Brother Perfect Lawton had turned around in the driver's seat. I jumped. The Sisters had stopped smiling.

Pointing at me with his thumb, he said to them, "You did

very well today with your assignment. Take an hour of contemplation time."

The Brother and the two Sisters practically fell out of the car mumbling, "Thank you, thank you. Yes, BP Lawton, yes, BP Lawton." I tried to follow them, but Brother Perfect Lawton put his hand on my arm.

"You and I, Little Sister, are going to the Big House. A great honor is being bestowed upon you, our newest member. Daddy Perfect himself is going to welcome you into the fold." He stepped on the gas and almost ran over three workers as he sped up the driveway toward the house on top of the hill.

Just before we reached the fence surrounding the house, we passed another large and elaborate building. Brother Perfect Lawton gestured at it and said, "That is the home of the First-Class Helpers, first and best assistants to Daddy Perfect."

"How many First-Class Helpers share the house?" I asked, noting to myself that there was a telephone line running to it.

"First-Class MEN," emphasized Brother Perfect Lawton. "At the moment, there is only myself. But, of course, with the passage of time, others will reach my spiritual heights and come live here on the mountain."

"And how about the First-Class Women, where do they live?"

"Down the hill—over there. They share their quarters with the Premium-Grade Women," he answered, pointing to another very large but not quite so elaborate house.

"Are there many First-Class Women?" I asked.

"Two, right now. They serve as assistants to MP—Mommy Perfect. They also supervise the Premium-Grade Women in the most important duty—cooking for the entire Perfect Family."

"The Perfect Family? They cook for the entire Brotherhood?" I asked.

64

"Don't be ridiculous. I mean, of course not, Little Sister. The Elevated Women prepare meals for Daddy Perfect's actual family. It includes Daddy Perfect, Mommy Perfect, Sonny Perfect I, Sonny Perfect II and Grandma Perfect, Daddy Perfect's blessed mother—when she is here. They all live in the Big House—except for Grandma Perfect, who lives in a condo in Palm Beach, Florida.

"I think all your questions will be answered in time. Just enjoy the privilege that you are about to experience. Most candidates—indeed most members of the Brotherhood—do not get a chance to visit Daddy and Mommy Perfect in their home."

I must have had a strange expression on my face because he quickly added, ". . . not until they have walked up a few of the Steps of Spirituality, at any rate. The climb purifies the uncleanliness of their souls. No Temple member would care to shed Spiritual Dirt in the home of our Sainted Parents."

"Oh," I said. "Then how come I'm being allowed into the house?"

Brother Perfect Lawton, First Class, ignored my question. We were passing through a second set of electrified gates. Two guards—cult members in light blue jumpsuits with royal blue belts—looked into the car and waved us on. Each wore a large black holster. Each holster contained a gun.

"They wouldn't hesitate to lay down their lives for the Perfect Family." BP Lawton saluted the guards in a military way.

"There are always two loyal brothers on guard in front of these gates," continued Brother Lawton. "Each does a twelve-hour shift. It is one of the most prized jobs in the Garden of Perfection—making sure the Agents of our Enemies do not harm the Perfects."

The guns frightened me. I had known there would be danger in this mission, but I had not thought about guns. I forced my mind to record all I was seeing—the location of buildings, guards, gates, guns. . . . My head was getting very full. I really needed my detecting notebook badly.

The house was enormous. We walked up a wide flight of marble steps to double wooden doors about twelve feet high. It felt like we were about to enter a church, or maybe a large theater. I had to hand it to Daddy Perfect—it was impressive.

The door was opened by what I assumed was a Premium-Grade Sister. She smiled at us.

I spoke. "Hello, Sister."

The smile left her face. She stood up very tall. Through stiff lips, she snarled at me, "An IMP does NOT address a Premium Grade unless she is spoken to. Who is your Group Leader? And what are you doing here? Why aren't you in your Rags of Righteousness?"

"An IMP? Group Leader? Rags of Righteousness? I'm here with Brother Lawton," I answered, gesturing to BP Lawton, First Class, who had stopped to talk to a worker at the bottom of the steps.

She seemed to get angrier. "Brother Perfect Lawton, First Class, to you, IMP. You ALWAYS address your superiors by their full Sacred Titles." She was red in the face and almost shouting. "And why haven't you memorized my name? All the names of the First Classes and Premium Grades should be committed to memory by all IMPs. . . ."

Brother Perfect Lawton, First Class, stepped in front of me. He glared at her. She shut up.

"You have a very big mouth, Enid. Close it and keep it closed." BP's voice was filled with poisonous sound. Sister Perfect Enid, Premium Grade, seemed to shrink. We walked into the entry hall—which could have been used as a Hollywood movie set.

Sister Perfect Enid led us into a large, luxurious office. She seated us in comfortable chairs before backing out of the room.

Brother Perfect Lawton, First Class, smiled his horrible smile at me. "While we're waiting for Daddy Perfect, I will explain a few things about our Brotherhood to you."

I sat back in my chair and returned the smile. "I'm really anxious to learn more," I said. For once, I was telling the absolute truth.

# 20

While we waited for Daddy Perfect to appear, Brother Perfect Lawton, First Class, began to describe life in the Temple of Perfection Brotherhood. As he spoke, I compared my observations to his words. Despite the smiling faces and BP Lawton's account of things, life in the Garden of Perfection did not appear to be carefree or happy or democratic. Brother Lawton had hardly gotten into his first major point —Dressing for Perfection, the sacred meaning attached to the clothing worn by different members of the cult—when Daddy Perfect entered the room abruptly. BP Lawton leaped to his feet and dragged me to mine. He bowed from the waist. I just stood there and despite my intentions, I shuddered.

Daddy Perfect strode across the room and stood in front of a big window. He raised his arms high, and the huge, flowing sleeves of his robe looked for a moment like wings unfolding. Because the sun was so bright behind him, I couldn't quite see the features of his face once he got in place. The light illuminated his hair in such a way that beams of brightness seemed to be radiating from his head. I wondered how long he had taken to work out just the right combination of dye job, light and wardrobe to create what I saw before me— Daddy Perfect, Unearthly Being.

"Hello, NP Cynthia, our newest member. Daddy Perfect

welcomes you. Daddy Perfect loves you. Please approach Daddy Perfect so he might bestow his blessing upon you." Speaking in a deep, booming voice, Daddy Perfect nodded to me.

"NP Cynthia?" I asked, walking toward him slowly.

"Shhhhhh!" whispered BP Lawton. "Nobody speaks to Daddy Perfect without permission."

"No, no, Brother Lawton. Let the little one speak if she so desires. Today we waive formalities." I was right in front of Daddy Perfect's desk.

All this time, Daddy Perfect had been standing with his arms outstretched. Now he lowered them slowly, placing his hands on the desktop. He leaned forward. His face came very close to mine. His hair was still lit up from behind. He smiled. He gave me a penetrating look.

"Daddy Perfect rejoices for you because it is through the Temple of Perfection and ONLY through the Temple of Perfection that you will ever get God's True Blessing. Daddy Perfect has a little paper for you to sign so you can immediately take your first step away from the ungraced state of Not Perfecthood. Sign this, Little Sister, and Daddy Perfect will enter your name into the Permanent Books of the Blessed."

I have always disliked and mistrusted people who talk about themselves in the third person. Daddy Perfect's little welcome forced my nutritionally starved brain cells to go on superalert. This was a dangerous man.

Daddy Perfect pulled a paper from a desk drawer. He slid it toward me and handed me a pen. "Sign, Little Sister. Sign on the dotted line and join The Brotherhood. IMPhood is about to be yours!"

"IMPhood? What is IMPhood? What is NP, for that matter? And what am I signing?" I figured that not to resist would be out of character and would cause DP to become suspicious.

Daddy Perfect sat down, leaned back in his chair and put

his feet up on the desk. "NP is what you are right now. It is the disgusting state lived in by most of the world. It is the ultimate degradation. It is Not Perfecthood. When you sign this seemingly insignificant paper, you will instantly become an IMP, The Brotherhood's affectionate term for a slightly more advanced state of being—Imperfecthood. You will be on the first step of the Journey to Perfecthood."

I picked up the piece of paper and began to read it. Daddy Perfect was on his feet. His winglike arms were in the air, flapping. "STOP!" he shouted. I stopped. As a matter of fact, I froze. He was pretty frightening.

"When Daddy Perfect tells you to sign something, you sign it. You must learn to trust your Daddy Perfect. He knows what is best for all his children. Now, Little Sister, sign the paper for Daddy. Show him you trust him with all your heart." Daddy Perfect had lowered one winged arm and placed a hand on my head in a kind of blessing. As he spoke, he pressed my head downward so it was looking at the legal paper. Before I signed, I was able to skim over some of the fine print. I picked up isolated words and phrases—*power of attorney, bequest, sound mind and body, all my worldly goods.*

I signed my name: *Cynthia Vanderbelt.*

Daddy Perfect whisked the paper from me. "That's a good little IMP. Daddy knows you feel better already. Now go with Brother Lawton to the IMP quarters. Blessings on you, little IMP, blessings." Daddy Perfect turned away from me.

BP Lawton grabbed my shoulder and pulled me out of the room. He walked backwards, and I stumbled sideways. When we got to the Rolls-Royce, he pushed me into the front seat next to him. On my way down the hill, he did not talk to me. All his friendliness was gone. It was almost as if I were invisible. An expected development.

BP Lawton stopped the car in front of a long, single-storied, wooden building. "Get out here, Cynthia. This is the female

IMP dormitory. Your Group Leader is Sister AP Clara. She's waiting for you inside." BP Lawton didn't even give me a chance to close the car door. He just pulled away and let it slam by itself as he made a fast U-turn. I faced the building. It was grim. It looked a little like buildings I had seen in old movies about World War II prison camps.

I walked up to the door, and as I knocked on it, someone jerked it open. "You must be the kid with all the money. Well, well, they should be celebrating up at the Big House just about now. You might as well come on in and get your rags. Life can't be wasted in sloth and idleness. Work, work. Yessiree. Let's get you settled. Move. Move. Close the door behind you. Flies get in. Mosquitoes, too. Goodness knows the path is difficult. Walk. Walk. . . ."

I followed the short, white-haired woman into the dormitory. She seemed completely insane but very likable. Words poured out of her mouth just about as fast as they must have popped into her head.

"Brother Lawton told me your name is Sister Clara."

Sister AP Clara turned to me. Her absolutely straight short hair bobbed as she talked. "Brother Perfect Lawton, First Class. IMPs and Almost Perfects must always address and refer to First Classes and Premium Grades and even ordinary Perfects by their full and earned titles. Of course, we break the rules amongst ourselves, but never let any of THEM overhear you doing it.

"Yes, Clara is my name—my own name—given to me by my beloved mother. I wouldn't change it for one million smackeroos. It means bright and shining, it does. Love my name. I figure God knows who I am, so why go through the hocus-pocus with that silly man on the hill."

"Who would make you change your name? What hocus-pocus? Silly man on the hill? Do you mean Daddy Perfect?" I asked excitedly. Who was this nice old lunatic?

"Did I say that? Goodness, goodness. I'm always shooting my mouth off. Ignore most of what I say except for the Rules, girl. I'm here to explain the Rules. Nobody listens to much else of what old Clara has to say, don't you know. Now let's get you a bed out of the draft."

I didn't know how many group leaders there were, but I was sure I had lucked out. Clara was crazy, but obviously Clara was not a brain-twisted follower of DP. Why was she there? I followed her down the row of beds. I counted twenty —ten on each side of the long room. Only seven were made up. I wondered which one belonged to Myra.

# 21

"This bed will be yours. Not too far from the bathroom." Clara was pointing to a bed exactly in the middle of a long row of identical metal beds. It, like all the other beds, was lined up under a small, glassless, screened window opening.

"Of course, you'll have to find some plastic to put over the window in winter so you don't catch pneumonia—but it's better than sleeping in the street. A garbage bag stuffed with dry leaves nailed in front of the opening really does the job. You look bright—you'll survive. On the other hand, you're here—a rich kid—so who knows? Maybe you aren't that bright. . . ."

Clara talked as she flipped down the thin, folded mattress on my new bed and walked over to a closet. It was held closed by a large combination lock. Clara spun the dial, opened the door and took out a blanket, two sheets, a pillow and a pillow-case. She kept mumbling to herself as she helped me make up the bed. I interrupted her.

"Why do you keep the bed linen locked up, Sister AP Clara? With the gates and guards, who would come in here to steal?"

Clara hiked her long skirt up to her knees and sat down on the bed. She patted the mattress with her hand, indicating that I should join her. I sat down, too.

"Look, rich kid, don't expect things to make much sense around here. Once you came through those gates, you entered a world that resembles a plate of eggs." Clara started giggling.

"A plate of eggs?" I asked.

"Scrambled." Clara kept giggling. Then she began laughing. Before I knew it, she was rocking back and forth with tears of joy coming out of her eyes. I didn't see what was so funny, but Clara got to me.

I began giggling, then laughing, and then the both of us were holding our sides and rocking back and forth. After a while, the laughter subsided. I felt so good. I hadn't realized how nervous and tense I had been.

"You needed that, didn't you, rich kid?" Clara was wiping her eyes with the corner of her skirt.

"Yes, I really did. Thank you, Sister AP Clara."

"Cut that out."

"Cut what out?"

"Cut the *Sister* garbage out. I'm old enough to be your grandmother. I'm not related to anyone here—and those stupid titles. Almost PURRfect; PURRfect, Premium Grade; PURRfect, First Class—sounds like the meat counter in a supermarket, doesn't it?" Clara drawled.

"Garden of PURRfection." She giggled. "Ha! Starting on the Path toward PURRfection, are you? Hee hee! Better wear high rubber boots—you're going to have to wade through a whole lot of manure."

I liked Clara. I wondered how much of her behavior was just an act. I decided I had to find out. "Clara, I need your help," I whispered.

I was taking a big chance. Maybe Clara was some kind of Temple of Perfection trick. Maybe she was a clever spy. Maybe she really was too crazy to trust, but I had no one else to turn to. Under the lunacy, Clara seemed to have a pretty clear view of the TOP.

Clara's laughter stopped abruptly. She looked totally sane. Quietly she said to me, "Don't whisper, it looks suspicious, but talk very softly. I knew the minute I saw you that you were not the usual recruit. Since yesterday, all that the high mucky-muck cultniks have talked about is the fortune of some kid—a Vanderbilt orphan."

"VanderBELT," I corrected.

"VanderBELT?" Clara snorted. "Nice twist. What's your scam, Cynthia—or whoever you are?"

"I won't tell you until you tell me who you are. Why are YOU here? You don't appear to believe a single thing Daddy Perfect teaches. Also, how did you know I wasn't a real IMP?"

"So many questions from such a pipsqueak. OK, whoever you are, fair is fair. I spotted you for a thinking person because (a) you lacked the sickening smirking smile, (b) you moved with energy like a real kid and (c) your eyes were alive.

"Of course, I don't believe the hocus-pocus. I take pride in the fact that I'm crazy, but I'm also very smart. Except for job assignments, recruits don't listen to a word I say—nobody does. But every once in a while, someone wakes up and decides to go home."

"People who are unhappy can just leave?" I almost shouted.

"Shhh," said Clara. "Of course not. Nobody is allowed to leave here without MP's permission—and she's a tyrant. All I said is that some DECIDE to go home. Making a decision and acting upon it are two entirely different kettles of fish. Folks get away from the Garden eventually, but eventually is usually a very long time—sometimes years if the high mucky-mucks even suspect you want to defect. I hate to be the one to break it to you, rich kid, but as long as you are an IMP, you're virtually a slave."

"Who are you, Clara?" I asked.

"I am what you might call a career shopping-bag lady. I lived on the streets and in train stations. I slept on the sidewalks of many a city—north and south, east and west—my worldly goods at my side at all times. I was an adventurer. I was free. I was unencumbered.

"Unfortunately, as the years passed, I found myself in the wrong place during the wrong season more and more. I found myself in Florida in August and in New York in January. My ability to float with the seasons was warping. I roasted in summer and nearly froze to death a couple of times in winter. Most disturbing of all, I was hungry more and more of the time. I was seriously contemplating a career change.

"One day I wandered past one of the Temple of Perfection thrift shops. I went in to get warm. I hung around and listened. I watched them recruit nitwits and geniuses—big and small. I saw the answer to my dilemma—a way out of the weather. Instead of a complete career change, I would just make a career alteration.

"You can guess that I wasn't exactly the kind of candidate the culties wanted—I was poor, I was old and, lacking the proper bathing facilities, I was temporarily extremely dirty. However, I was also very persistent. I devoted my complete and total energy to the project.

"I came back, day after day, for two months. Finally, not knowing what else to do with me, they signed me up. So here I am.

"Nobody bothers me much. In fact, nobody pays any attention to me at all, including the IMPs—which suits me just fine. I get my own room, three meals a day, plus my own hot plate, so I can have tea whenever I want. In return, I teach the Rules to newcomers, and I never make a fuss in meetings."

"Don't you have family, Clara?" I asked, taking her hand.

"Nope. No family. Besides, most of the time, I'm crazy as a loon. Where else could I live and not be locked away?"

"But you are locked away, Clara. You are surrounded by electrified fences and guards."

"I know how to get out of here whenever I want. I'm not locked in, the rest of the world is locked out."

"Do you mean that, Clara? You know how to get out of here?" I only half believed her. Maybe Clara was hallucinating.

"Sure, but why would I want to leave? Where would I go?"

"Would you help someone else leave if they desperately wanted to get out?"

"Your turn to talk, Cynthia Vanderbelt—imposter." Clara clamped her lips shut and stared at me.

# 22

"I'm not really an heiress," I began.

"So what else is new?" asked Clara.

Working up my nerve because I figured if Clara blew my cover I would be in big trouble, I told her who I was and from whom I was descended. She was impressed. Finally, I admitted that I was on an important case—the rescue of my older sister.

"Oh, goody, an adventure! High adventure and mystery! A caper of magnificent proportions! An altruistic romp! A rescue of a damsel in distress! Hee hee!" Clara seemed to like the idea of my rescuing my sister a whole lot.

"And what is the young woman's name? And how on earth

did a sister of yours, an honest-to-goodness descendent of that great man Holmes, get caught by the Perfect clan? Ho ho!"

Clara was having a wonderful time. I was happy that she was happy. She didn't seem to mind one bit that I was about to reduce the membership of the TOP by two—Myra and myself.

"Her name is Myra."

Clara stopped looking happy. "No fooling? Myra? That one? The one who came in yesterday? She's YOUR sister? Sheeesh!"

"Do you know her?"

"Of course I know her. All female IMPs live here with me until they are promoted."

"Which is Myra's bed? When will she be back here?" I didn't want to shock Myra with my presence. Considering the mood she had been in during our last conversation, I was sure she would turn me in.

"Over there," said Clara, pointing to a bed with a folded bare mattress on it. "And she won't be back today. Sorry, small detective, but you had better just work at getting your own butt out of here. Myra is a lost cause, the little jerk!"

I got angry and a little scared at the same time. "Don't call my sister a jerk, Clara—and why is her bed unmade? Has something horrible happened to her?"

"But she is a jerk. She's a bimbo. She's spoiled. She is a huge pain in the neck. And, for your information, her extreme jerkitude has gotten her thrown into jail in less than twenty-four hours. Give up, Detective Holmes. Cut your losses, lick your wounds, go home!" Clara was shaking her head while she walked toward a cabinet.

"But Clara, what did she do?"

"Do? DO? What did she do? What didn't she do? What didn't she like? What didn't she say? Phooey! A real pain. She wanted her own room—didn't want to share it with the rest

76

of the IMPs. She wanted her own closet, special attention from the Perfects, and she said she was sorry she had given all her things to the 'stupid Temple of Perfection' because not only was this an imperfect place, it was low-class and horrible.

"She told this to EVERYONE! She refused to work, refused to call people by their proper titles and, at dinner last night, your sister Myra threw her plate across the room, saying that the food was fit only for a garbage can.

"The last I saw of her was this morning, when they carried her off the hill where she had run in an attempt to complain directly to Daddy Perfect. She was screaming and kicking when she was thrown into the House of Repentance."

"The House of Repentance?"

"The jail, detective kid. The jail. It's over near the Almost Perfect men's dormitory. Now put these things on and give me your street clothes."

I took a pair of patched, faded, blue overalls and a blue shirt from Clara. As I changed my clothing, I tried to clear my head. Myra had really done it again. Not only had she gotten herself locked behind eight-foot-high electrified fences patrolled by armed guards, but she had gotten herself thrown into jail as well. It was a terrible predicament. I needed time to case the place in daylight. I pulled on the badly fitting shirt and overalls and interrupted Clara, who was looking out the window and muttering to herself.

"Clara, I have to explore the compound. Do you assign IMP jobs?"

"Who else?" said Clara.

"Is there a job you could give me that would let me wander around a little—unnoticed?"

Clara thought for a minute. "Sure. But why should I help you?"

I couldn't think of an answer to that. Clara didn't know me. She had a home here that was much better than life on the streets. She received food and clothing, and nobody bothered her. There was no reason I could think of for Clara to jeopardize the life she had made for herself—none that would make much sense, at any rate. I was silent.

"Right," said Clara. "There is no rational reason for me to help you. Even a crazy old woman like me knows that. On the other hand, the loveliest thing about being crazy is that you never have to be rational. So I'll help you, detective kid. Take this bag and do a garbage patrol. If anyone asks you, tell them you are cleaning up the dirt which is spoiling the Perfectness of the Garden of Perfection. Return here on the run when you hear the Bells of Obedience. They'll ring five times."

"Clara, thank you. I think you are a terrific person."

"Tish tosh," said Clara, but she looked pleased. She held the door open for me, and I walked out into the Garden of Perfection.

As she closed it, she said, "The House of Repentance is next to the male IMP dormitory."

I kind of zigzagged toward two large, many-windowed, identical single-story buildings. I deduced that one long building was the dormitory and one was the jail. As I got close, I could see that one building had heavy wire mesh nailed over the windows. I had located the jail. Working my way toward one narrow end of it, I could see a guard standing at attention in front of a door. I backed off. I retraced my steps, bending and stooping, picking up an occasional twig and small pebble.

One side of the House of Repentance was very near the electrified fence which surrounded the grounds. I was able to examine the barrier carefully. It was nasty. The fence had barbed wire strung along its top. Branches which had once overhung it had been cut off. As an escape route, an attempted climb over the electrified fortress would be suicidal.

I continued to move around the building. The windows were about six feet off the ground, so I couldn't see in without standing on something and drawing attention to myself. I decided to leave the area and explore as much of the compound as possible before the Bells of Obedience were rung.

"Argggggghhhhhhhh. Oh NO. It's my sister! IT'S MY SISTER! SHERELEE. SHER-EL-EEEEEEEEEEEEE!"

I whirled around. Myra had her face pressed to the wire mesh at one of the windows. She was screaming in a high-pitched, hysterical way. My goose was cooked. I couldn't even run because where could I go? In another couple of minutes, I'd be locked in a cell alongside my jerk sister.

I tried to signal her to shut up. She kept screaming. I heard running footsteps. The guard appeared from around the front of the building. He had his gun drawn. I dropped my garbage bag.

"What's going on here? Who are you? What is she screaming about? Why are you here? Answer me, IMP!" He was a mean-looking kid not too much older than Myra.

"I'm Sister Cynthia, sir," I said, staring at his gun.

"You're new here, aren't you, IMP scum?"

"Yes, sir. Today is my first day."

"You're supposed to call me Brother. Brother AP Rodney. You'll learn. Why is she screaming?"

Myra hadn't stopped shooting off her mouth for a single second. Now that he had gotten the information he wanted from me, Brother AP Rodney was listening to Myra.

"SHE'S MY SISTER! SHE'S MY LITTLE SISTER. GET ME OUT OF HERE, SHERELEE! DON'T YOU UNDERSTAND? SHE'S MY SISTER!"

Brother Almost Perfect Rodney smiled up at Myra and responded, "Good, Sister Myra. That's good progress. Of course, she's your Sister. And I am your Brother. A few more days of that kind of progress, and you'll be done with your repenting. Our little talks are succeeding. Praise Daddy!"

"No, you don't understand, you boring little twirp! That

girl standing next to you . . . IS MY *REAL* SISTER! IT'S SHERELEE! MY *ACTUAL* SISTER!" At that moment, I wished Myra would fall through a hole in the floor. I wanted to kill her.

However, luck was with me, because Brother AP Rodney said, "Yes, yes, she is your REAL Sister. You are finally getting it. You are putting your feet on the Path. We are ALL real Brothers and Sisters in The Brotherhood."

Myra was getting more and more hysterical. She had her fingers wrapped around the wire mesh and was shaking it as hard as she could. "YOU ARE AN IDIOT, RODNEY. THAT IS MY SISTER. WHY DON'T YOU UNDERSTAND? THAT IS MY SISTER SHERELEE! SHERELEE. SHERELEE. SHERELEE. SHERELEE."

I gave Rodney an embarrassed look. He shrugged his shoulders and shouted up to Myra so he could be heard over her screams. "You should address me as Brother AP Rodney, Sister Myra. Little slips like that help earn you demerits and hamper your progress along the Path—you know that. And this Little Sister's name is Cynthia. CYNTHIA!"

"NOOOOOOOOOOOOO!" screeched Myra.

"YESSSSSSSSSSS!" shouted Rodney, waving his gun in the air.

Myra made that noise again. "Arggggggggggghhhhhhh." Her head disappeared from the window. I could hear her sobbing. It did not sound like an act.

"What a flake," said Brother AP Rodney. "My first prisoner, and she has to be a real jerk. Now get back to work and learn a lesson from this." I waited for a minute to hear what the lesson might be, but Brother AP Rodney didn't seem to have anything else to say. He holstered his pistol, smiled that now-familiar smile at me and marched back to his post.

The bells began to ring. The Bells of Obedience sounded

just like someone ringing a doorbell over a public-address system. As I was running back to the IMP quarters, the sound followed me. I noticed loudspeakers hanging in many of the trees.

I dropped my garbage bag on top of a pile of garbage bags which had appeared in front of the barracks. I ran in the door. Each IMP was standing in front of a made-up bed. I ran to my bed and joined the lineup. There were eight of us. Two were about my mother's age, one looked about twenty-five and the rest were older teenagers. I was the only kid-type there. I reminded myself that I told them I was fourteen and a few months.

There was no conversation. Not a single person acknowledged that there was a new IMP in their midst. I sat down on my bed and nodded to Clara. She ignored me. I wondered if Myra's outburst was going to be my undoing.

# 23

Clara thumbtacked a hand-lettered poster to the wall behind her. It said:

MOMMY KNOWS BEST
AND SHE SAYS
CLEANLINESS IS NEXT TO PERFECTNESS!

CLEANLINESS IS THE SUREST PATH TO HEAVEN.
CLEAN IS AS CLEAN DOES.
THERE IS NO SUCH THING AS TOO CLEAN.
DIRT IS THE OPIATE OF THE PEOPLE.
A WASH IN TIME SAVES NINE.
BETTER DEAD THAN DIRTY.

As each IMP noticed the sign, her smile seemed to get less bright. Some of the IMPs began examining their fingernails.

"Mommy's coming to visit us, ladies. You have exactly ten minutes to get yourselves ready," announced Clara. Everyone rushed to the back of the bunkhouse. I joined them, although I didn't feel very dirty.

The small bathroom only had two sinks in it. Three women were crowded around each one—frantically scrubbing their faces and hands. The others were pushing and shoving to get into the room. I waited for the crowd to clear out. I finally made my way to a sink and had just soaped my hands when I heard a whistle blast. The girl next to me was drying her face. She dropped the towel and poked me.

"Let's go, Sister. Mommy's coming."

I began to rinse off my hands, but the girl grabbed my arm and pulled me into the large room.

"You don't want to be late when Mommy visits," she whispered. We ran to our beds. I wiped my hands on my coveralls.

Things were getting stranger and stranger. The only one in the room besides me who wasn't nervously cleaning nails or combing hair was Clara. She stood at the front of the room staring into space and humming to herself.

The door slammed open. All the Sisters jumped to their feet and stood at attention. Naturally, I joined them.

"MOMMY'S HERE!" shouted a tall woman in an ankle-length blue robe as she strode into the room. "ATTENTION!" she commanded.

The already stiff-standing people in the room became even stiffer—sucking in stomachs and tucking in chins. Except Clara. She shuffled off to the side of the room and leaned against a wall. A second tall, blue-robed woman marched into the room and glared at Clara. Clara, staring into space, didn't seem to notice.

A bent-over woman backed through the door. She was

dragging a large, wooden, high-backed armchair. She was puffing and sweating. I began to take a step forward to help her when I noticed Clara staring at me. She was shaking her head. I filed another important piece of information. Clara was nowhere near as unconscious as she let the other cult members believe.

"Spiritual dirt," someone whispered.

I looked in the direction of the whisper. It was the girl who had dragged me away from the sink.

"Don't look at me," she hissed.

I turned away. "Spiritual dirt?" I whispered back.

"IMPs are not allowed to touch Mommy's sacred chair because we'll soil it with our spiritual dirt."

"Oh," I whispered, not really understanding.

Then the whole roomful of people seemed to take a deep breath and hold it. Mommy Perfect moved into the room slowly. She glided down the aisle of IMPs. Her shimmering blue robe touched the floor so you couldn't see her feet. The way she moved made it seem as if she were floating inches above the ground. Mommy Perfect's white-blond hair was pulled back from her face so precisely that it almost looked painted onto her skull.

Mommy Perfect stopped briefly in front of each IMP in the row opposite me. Each one held out her hands for inspection and then turned her head and bent back her ears so Mommy Perfect could inspect behind them. Mommy Perfect nodded her head once after the ear check and then appeared to float to the next bed. Each inspected IMP sighed and got a dreamy look on her face. The little cult smile returned to lips.

Finishing that row, Mommy Perfect started up my row. In it, one IMP did not meet her standards and was given a demerit. I had been feeling nervous about this inspection, but hearing the punishment, I relaxed. Big deal. A demerit.

Mommy Perfect stopped in front of me. I held out my

hands as I had seen the others doing. Mommy Perfect glanced at them and got a look of disgust on her face. Before I could bend back my ears, Mommy Perfect grabbed my chin with her perfectly manicured hand. She turned my head to the left and to the right. Then, holding on so tight that I could feel her fingers digging into my chin bone, she stared right into my eyes. This was a terrifying woman.

Her eyes were the pale ice blue of a glacier. The carefully applied bright blue eye shadow and long, blue false lashes made them seem unreal—like the eyes of a giant doll which has come to life and gone mad. Her polished fingernails were long, tapered and very red. Despite my fear, I tried smiling. Unfortunately, my effort was wasted by the pressure of her very strong fingers on my cheeks. She was squashing my mouth. My smile was turned into a fishlike expression.

"Why are you making faces at your Mommy Perfect, IMP?" she snarled.

I tried speaking, but she was still holding onto my face.

"No one speaks to Mommy Perfect unless spoken to first," shouted one of the blue-robed women.

I had been spoken to and I said so, but not having free use of my mouth, the words came out as meaningless sounds.

Mommy Perfect let go of me. "This IMP is a disgusting, dirty disgrace to our Garden of Perfection. Wash her, handmaidens. Show her the glory of cleanliness. Then bring her to me."

Before I could object, I was grabbed under the elbows by the two tallest handmaidens and carried to the bathroom. Once there, one held my arms in a sink while the other soaped my hands, arms, neck and face thoroughly. Then, taking a rough washcloth and a stiff nailbrush from a pocket in her robe, the soaper began scrubbing me. It hurt. I tried to pull away, but the other woman held me.

"Rinse her. Mommy's waiting," said the Sister holding me.

They ran hot water over my arms and then pushed my head close to the sink. Water was sloshed over my head. It washed away the soap and soaked my hair. I closed my eyes and wasn't prepared for the towel being wrapped around my entire head—face included. The Sisters dried my arms and hands while I stood, blinded by the head wrap. Then suddenly one of them announced, "Clean as an IMP can be."

The other one answered, "Let us hope so."

I wondered to myself why anyone would want to be part of this cult. So far, it was a very unpleasant experience. Why did everyone go around smiling most of the time? I remained silent and was carried back to Mommy Perfect and set down in front of her. She was sitting in the armchair.

"That's better, handmaidens. A job well done. Stand aside while I talk to this blessed new Little Sister."

Blessed new Little Sister? I thought. A few minutes before, I had been a disgusting, dirty disgrace. What about demerits? The IMP with the less-than-perfect fingernail got demerits—and I had been forced to practically take a bath in a sink. Seconds before, I had been sure I would be thrown in jail with Myra.

Mommy Perfect smiled at me. She patted my cheek gently. I could hear sighs of envy and pleasure behind me, coming from the other IMPs.

"Dear Little Sister Cynthia. I regret the harshness of this treatment you have just received, but Mommy was unaware that this was your very first day in the Garden of Perfection. Do you forgive your Mommy?"

"Ohhhhhhhhhhh," everyone behind me said.

"Why not?" I said. It was obvious that Mommy Perfect had found out who I was while I was getting scrubbed. The Perfects wanted to make little Cynthia Vanderbelt as happy as possible. I felt better. For the time being, Cynthia's millions would protect me—I hoped.

"Very good, dear little IMP. Mommy loves you. Mommy loves all of you." Mommy Perfect turned her ice-blue eyes to the group behind me.

"Ahhhhhhhhhhhh," they said.

"Do you all love your Mommy?"

"We love you, Mommy," they all responded. I was still facing Mommy Perfect. I could see Clara leaning against a wall. She appeared to have fallen asleep on her feet. Her mouth was slightly open, her chin was resting on her chest, and I thought I could hear quiet snores coming from her corner of the room.

"And WHO IS MOMMY PERFECT?" Mommy Perfect continued.

Everyone except Clara and me answered in unison, "You are Mommy Perfect, the Avenger, the Enforcer, the Right Hand of Daddy Perfect. You keep us on the Perfect Path."

"And do you REALLY love your Perfect Mommy?"

"We REALLY, REALLY love our Perfect Mommy."

Mommy Perfect smiled at me again—with her mouth. Her eyes remained hard and cold. I smiled back—the little cult smile I had been practicing.

"Return to your bed, Child of Perfection. And never forget the lesson you learned today."

I turned to walk away and was grabbed again by a tall handmaiden. "Backwards," she hissed. "Always leave Mommy and Daddy backwards." She whirled me around. I stumbled toward my bed—walking backwards.

Mommy Perfect stood up. "Honor Mommy!" a hand-maiden shouted.

All the IMPs dropped facedown, flat onto the floor. I did as they did. There were the sounds of footsteps and the chair being dragged and the slamming of the door and, finally, a whistle blast. The IMPs got to their feet.

"Free time until we leave for the dining hall," announced Clara. Most of the IMPs flopped onto their beds. A few began talking excitedly to each other—looking over their shoulders at me every once in a while. I didn't like the attention. It's difficult for a detective to operate efficiently while in the limelight.

"So, how come you rate special treatment, Cynthia?" The girl on the bed next to mine was smiling a genuine, noncult smile at me.

"Special treatment?" I asked.

"No demerits, no lockup, not even a hand slap—and by Mommy's standards, you were filthy."

"Maybe I was spared because it's my first day."

"No one is ever spared for any reason when it comes to Mommy Perfect and dirt. So who are you?"

"Who are you?" I answered, stalling.

"I asked first."

"So you did," I said.

# 24

"My name is Cynthia Vanderbelt," I said. The girl who was questioning me looked about eighteen years old. She was stuffed into a pair of overalls which seemed about two sizes too small for her. She had dark, short, curly hair and a genuinely friendly and intelligent expression on her pretty face. She was not smiling that little, smug, cult smile.

"That's not what I asked you. Who are you?"

"I don't know what you are talking about," I said. What had I done to blow my cover? Was this chubby, seemingly innocent IMP next to me a cult spy? Had they planted her there to pump me for information? All my sharp Holmes instincts were on the alert.

"Sure you do. What are you doing in the old Garden of

87

Perfection, clean capital of the world?" The girl began laughing.

"What's your name?" I asked, trying to change the subject.

"Jane Doe."

"Baloney," I said.

"It's as good as Cynthia Vanderbelt," she answered, winking at me.

"Look, Cynthia Vanderbelt is my name. If you don't want to tell me your name, that's just fine with me." I was losing my cool detective control.

"Jane is my real name. Jane Brady. And Cynthia Vanderbelt may be your name, but I doubt it—and I would bet just about anything that you're not here to join the Temple of Perfection. You just proved it."

"What do you mean?" My palms were beginning to sweat.

Jane leaned toward me and began whispering. "I mean, you do not have the foggy, otherworldly look in your eyes that other first-day IMPs always have. You are not oozing feelings of harmony and love from your every pore. You actually got angry at me a moment ago instead of smiling and wandering off."

"Why would I wander off?" I whispered back at her.

"To avoid conflict. The lower orders of the Temple are conditioned to avoid conflict. Also, to report me for bugging you." Jane had stopped smiling.

"Lower orders?" I asked.

"We're the lowest. We do all the dirtiest, most boring work around here. We're told that we are working our way up the Ladder of Perfection. Actually, it's slave labor."

Why was she telling me all of this? She had to be a spy. Maybe Myra's outburst had alerted the Perfects.

"If it's all so bad, why are you here?" I asked coldly, as if I were offended by what she had just said.

"Because I got caught—tricked—duped. I was an idiot." Jane suddenly looked miserable. "I was in college—my first term there. I was lonely, hundreds of miles away from home and a whole lot fatter than I am now. Nobody ever asked me out for a date. Nobody seemed to care that I was bright and nice and interesting. I spent all my time reading, eating and being unhappy.

"Then one day, in the library, a guy sat down next to me. He began talking to me and wound up asking me out for coffee. He told me about these people who just loved and respected each other—who had found a way to live where everyone was happy and content. He invited me to a meeting at the Nearly Perfect Shoppe. And here I am."

"How long have you been here?" I asked.

"Two and a half awful months."

"Awful?" I was still suspicious. Why was this almost adult person confiding in a stranger—a very young stranger?

"Horrible. I hate it here. The first couple of weeks were just fine—I felt as if I were part of the most loving group in the world. I was special. We were special. Nothing bothered me —and then something happened inside my head."

"What?" I was really curious.

"It was like waking up from a dream. One day I looked around, and it all looked different to me. It felt different. I don't know why. Nothing special had happened. I was sitting in the meeting hall listening to Daddy Perfect speak, and it all seemed alien. The happy people around me seemed mindless and robotlike. I didn't belong anymore." Jane stopped speaking.

"Then why are you still here?" I asked.

"How can I leave?"

"Are you broke? Is that the problem?"

"No. I could call my parents, and they would even pick me up."

"So, what's your problem? Why are you still here?" I was getting impatient.

"How can I leave?" Jane looked ready to cry.

"You said that already. What do you mean, Jane? You just walk out. Tell them you are fed up and want to leave."

"You think it's that simple? If I told anyone I wanted to leave the Temple, I would be thrown into the House of Repentance until I changed my mind.

"A new girl, a real jerk, got thrown in there last night. I think she broke some kind of record for getting locked up."

"I know." The words just slipped out of my mouth.

"I know you know," Jane answered. "I overheard you talking to her and the dim-witted guard."

"She's just some crazy nut, that's all," I said.

"She may be crazy, and she may be a nut and, in my opinion, she is also obnoxious—but she is your real sister— isn't she, Sherelee?"

I stared at Jane. It was a shock hearing my real name whispered in that place. Myra's big mouth had sunk us both. I couldn't remember Great-great-grandpa Sherlock ever having been in as tight a spot.

# 25

I was temporarily saved by the Bells of Obedience, which had begun to ring over the PA system. Clara blew two ear-splitting blasts on her whistle, and the IMPs began forming a line down the center of the room. I got behind Jane.

"No, no, IMP Cynthia," called Clara. "Size places. Everything neat and orderly. Come to the front of the line." I was separated from curious Jane, the possible stool pigeon, because I was short.

"Follow me," said Clara, and we all marched out the door, down the steps, across the compound and into a huge building

90

which turned out to be one gigantic room. There was a stage and chairs set up at one end of it. Toward the middle, long tables were neatly lined up in rows. We stopped. No one moved. Then someone blew a whistle.

Everyone scattered—except me. Brooms and dustrags appeared. Dishes clanked in the distance. Mops and pails of water were dragged out, and as each sweeper swept a patch of floor, a mopper followed to swab it down. The smell of disinfectant was so strong I almost gagged.

"Better follow me," said Clara, moving toward the far wall where IMP women were scurrying around a large kitchen area. A banner hung over the entryway.

### MOMMY SAYS EAT EVERYTHING OR ELSE!

"Work with Jane. She'll show you what to do." Clara wandered off. I wondered if Clara had been trying to give me some kind of message by assigning me to Jane. I tried to catch Clara's eye, but she was leaning against a wall seeming to stare into space.

I turned and said sweetly, "What do I do, Jane?"

"Help me get the instant mashed potatoes ready for mixing, Cynthia." Jane smiled at me.

We filled a huge pot with water and set it on the stove. Jane added three teaspoons of margarine and about a cup of salt to the pot.

"Stir that when the water begins to boil." Jane handed me a mixing spoon.

I did as directed, thinking that Jane must have made a mistake adding so much salt and so little margarine. I was stirring the bubbling, salty water and trying to decide what my next move would be when Jane walked over with a sack in her arms.

"Government-remaindered dehydrated potatoes," she said, dumping the contents of the sack into the cauldron. "Stir," she ordered. "And in case you think I made some stupid mistake by adding that much salt and almost no margarine— you're wrong. It's Mommy Perfect's orders I follow. Margarine is expensive, and Americans love salt. I once heard her tell a handmaiden that she could get this crowd to eat fried straw if she salted it enough."

"Look, why are you following me around telling me these things?" I asked. "Maybe I should report you. Yes, I think I'll go report you now—for subversion." I stood the wooden spoon in the almost solid mixture of potatoes and began to walk away.

Jane got very pale. "I don't know what your game is, Sherelee," she whispered, "but if this is some kind of test, I'm going to pass. They'll put me straight into jail. Will that make you happy?"

I stared at Jane for a full minute. I was sure she wasn't acting. Beads of sweat had appeared on her upper lip. She had tears in her eyes.

"I had to be sure, Jane. Is there ever any private time around here when we can talk?"

"We get fifteen minutes after dinner to digest our food. We can even go outside for a short walk."

"Have you made the gravy, IMPs?" An Almost Perfect woman wandered into the kitchen area. "Those potatoes look a bit solid to me. Add water to them."

I dumped a few cups of water into the rigid potatoes and tried to loosen them up a little. Jane heated water in another enormous pot and then dumped the contents of a labelless box into it.

"More food rejected by the U.S. government," she said, stirring vigorously.

There were three stoves in the kitchen area. At the other two, people seemed to be rehydrating some kind of meat and a vegetable. Because of the nature of the cooking, dinner was ready in a remarkably short time. Two of the male IMPs

92

carried the heavy pots to a long, low table. Each team of "cooks" stood behind their creations. Jane handed me an ice-cream scoop.

"Two scoops of potatoes on each plate—even if they beg you to skip it," she said.

"Why?" I asked.

"Mommy insists everyone finish everything on his or her plate. No exceptions. She knows that the cheap, surplus potatoes are even cheaper than bread. They are also very filling."

"I bet," I said, staring down into the horrible goo I had helped create.

People began straggling into the building. Cleaning tools were put away, and a line began to form near the food table. The IMPs, having already been there, were in the front of the line at first but kept getting pushed farther and farther back as Almost Perfects and Perfects arrived for the meal.

"They all eat this slop?" I whispered to Jane.

"Everyone but the Perfect Family and their personal hand-maidens. The Perfects eat gourmet meals. The handmaidens eat leftovers. It's a great honor to eat something which has actually been on Daddy Perfect's plate. If he's actually touched it—or, better yet, chewed it and spit it out, it becomes sacred." Jane had begun to giggle.

"You're kidding. That's gross."

"I wish I were kidding. As the Perfects come for their food, see how many of them are wearing little plastic bags on chains around their necks. There is a brisk business around here in food amulets."

"Yick," I said.

"Double yick," said Jane. "The Perfectionists are all here. Start dishing."

The line of hungry Brothers and Sisters, each carrying a metal plate, a fork, spoon and knife, began moving past us. I dropped two scoops of instant mashed potato onto each plate. Jane ladled a blob of lumpy instant gravy over each scoop. The next person dumped on the rehydrated chipped beef, which was sort of a gray color. Then came the spoonful of wrinkled peas. At the end of the table, each cultist took a single slice of white bread and a plastic cup of what looked like colored water.

"Is that juice?" I asked.

"Instant flavored sugar water—cheaper than juice."

"Do we have to eat this junk?"

The last two people were passing through the food line, and the potato pot was almost empty. We must have served fifty people.

Jane peered into the pot nervously. "I hope there's enough for all of the cooks."

"You want to eat this?" I asked.

"Don't be an idiot. Who would WANT to eat this stuff? It's required. Notice how no one is eating yet. They can't begin until we sit down with our plates. If our plates are less than full, we get into bad trouble. We'll be reported to Mommy Perfect for bad management—sloppy serving."

"Who would bother to report us?"

"Everyone who has to eat his fair share." Jane was scraping the bottom of the potato and gravy pots to make enough portions for the servers. Someone was doing the same with the beef and vegetables. They succeeded. We were all served. We trooped, smiling, to empty seats at a nearby table.

"BEGIN!" shouted a voice over the PA system. Everyone dug into his food. I had never seen a roomful of people eating so fast. I could hardly look at my plate, it was so horrible.

"Eat," said Jane with a full mouth. "Eat fast or else." She didn't stop chewing for a second.

I picked up my fork, held my breath and began shoveling in the food. The potatoes stuck to the roof of my mouth. Soon the chipped beef joined them. I picked up my plastic cup to wash it all down with sugar water, but Jane poked me. She

94

shook her head but couldn't speak, because her mouth was full.

I put down my glass and began to eat. A bell rang. People were using their bread to clean off their plates. They rubbed the plates until they shone.

"Hurry," Jane managed to gurgle. "That was the warning bell. Only two minutes before the end of the meal. You had better be finished."

I ate faster. I used the bread to clean the plate. Finally, just as everyone else was doing, I washed it all down with the pink water.

"Nice work for the first meal here," whispered Jane, wiping her mouth.

"Thanks," I said, hoping there would be no dessert.

"FINISH!" The voice shouted so loud that the empty plates on the tables jumped.

I looked around. I couldn't see a speck of food, a droplet of gravy, a morsel of leftover chipped beef on any plate within my sight.

"BREAK TIME," the public-address system squealed.

"Let's go outside," said Jane.

"Don't we have to clean the pots?" I asked.

"No, that's punishment duty for the people in jail."

"Oh," I said. Perhaps my luck has changed, and I have a break in the case at last, I thought.

# 26

"So why are you here?" asked Jane. We had wandered away from the building and the other people.

"What's it to you?" I asked. I was trying to memorize the terrain while we talked. It was beginning to get dark.

"I think you came here for a reason, and maybe that reason will help me get out of here."

"Interesting guess." I stared blankly at Jane.

"You are the strangest child I have ever met." Jane sounded frustrated.

"Don't call me a child. I resent it." I needed information from Jane, and we were wasting valuable minutes. I was about to get to the point when two armed guards marched by, telling us to move closer to the meeting hall. Myra wasn't the only prisoner in the Garden of Perfection.

I turned to Jane. "My name is Sherelee Holmes." I briefly told Jane who I was and why I was there. I crammed the entire story into about three minutes. Time was of the essence. When I finished, I took a deep breath.

"Oh, rats and spiders and other disgusting things," she said.

"I beg your pardon?" I said.

"You're a nut—a dingbat. Your marbles are so loose I can hear them rattling from here." Jane looked defeated.

"You're entitled to your opinion, Jane," I said, keeping a cool head and ignoring the insults. "But I need information. Are the dirty pots brought to the prisoners or are the prisoners brought to the pots? What time does all this happen? How many guards are assigned to the prisoners?"

"Ohhh, no. You can't snatch your sister from these geeks. Where will you take her? We'll all wind up in jail."

"Just answer my questions."

"Prisoners are brought to the pots—no sinks in the jail. It's done at midnight to keep the prisoners from sleeping too much. One guard to a prisoner. Your sister is the only one in jail right now." Then Jane sighed.

"Perfect." I smiled at Jane.

"Don't use that word around me."

"Sorry. A plan is forming in my astute mind." And it was —sort of.

A whistle blew.

"We have to go back now. It's time for your Perfect Experience."

"What's that?" I asked.

"Follow me," said Jane.

The tables we had used for eating were covered with cartons. The benches at the tables were beginning to fill with IMPs and Almost Perfects. The more senior-looking cult members were standing, arms folded, in a ring around the tables.

"Sit!" said Jane, pulling me onto a bench beside her.

A Perfect walked up to each table and flipped open the cartons. Some were filled with colored paper, and some with wire. Then the Perfect dumped a pile from each box in front of each of us.

"What do I do with this stuff, and what is it?" I asked.

"Shhhh," whispered Jane. "We make flowers, which are sold on the street and to gift shops."

"Why?" I whispered.

"The Perfects like money. A constant cash flow gives them great religious experiences."

"Do we get paid for doing this?"

"Come off it, Sherelee."

"Call me Cynthia." I glanced around to see if anyone had heard, but everyone was concentrating on making flowers.

"Sorry, I forgot." Jane's hands were flying. In those few moments, she had shaped red paper into a rose and was twisting green wire into a stem. The woman on my left had made two poppies, and the young man across from me had actually fashioned a very passable paper tulip.

I selected some yellow paper from my pile and got to work. In about ten minutes, I had produced three tattered messes with stems. I felt a hand on my shoulder. I looked up.

"Ah, in addition to being a filthy Little Sister, you also appear to be totally untalented." The fingers dug into my shoulder. It was one of the handmaidens who had washed me earlier.

"Sister!" The other handmaiden I had met pried the fingers from my shoulder. "Mommy says to treat this one nicely. She will learn to make the Perfect Flowers in time. Won't you, Little IMP Sister?" She smiled the cult smile at me. I smiled it back at her. They wandered off.

I grabbed some more paper strips and had just completed a multicolored, giant flower which could have starred in a horror movie—*The Flower That Ate Connecticut*—when the Bells of Obedience rang. All the workers neatly arranged their flowers in front of them, then sat quietly, hands folded in laps. A Perfect Brother with a clipboard walked around each table —stopping behind each flower producer and taking notes. When our Perfect Brother got to me, he sort of choked, then moved quickly to Jane. She had managed to make fifteen very nice flowers. The woman on the other side of me had produced at least twenty.

Having inspected the work, the Perfect Brother signaled an Almost Perfect Sister who circled the table collecting the completed flowers, which she deposited in a large florist's box. The materials were dumped back into the cartons, and another bell rang.

Everyone got up. Tables were pushed to the side wall and piled up. Benches were dragged to the stage area and placed behind chairs. The Perfect Brothers and Sisters filed to the front two aisles. The Almost Perfects sat behind them. We, the IMPs, sat on the benches.

A fanfare blared over the public-address system. Everyone stood as a voice boomed, "Rise and greet our Perfect Leader, our Daddy of the Spirit, our Exalted Guide and his Blessed Family!"

Brother Perfect Lawton, First Class, stood in front of the stage, off to one side. He held a microphone in his hand.

BP Lawton nodded his head, and everyone in the room except me began chanting. The lights went out in the entire meeting hall. About a minute passed. A bright spotlight lit up the center of the stage. Daddy Perfect was standing there, arms raised, winged sleeves flying, halo hair seeming to float around his head.

"OOOhhhhhhh," said almost everyone and continued chanting.

"He gets the same reaction every time," whispered Jane, "and he does this at least three times a week."

"It is impressive," I whispered back.

"Gets boring after a while," Jane mumbled.

I was able to see some faces in the reflected light. They were raptly staring at their beloved Daddy Perfect. "Not to them," I said, feeling a shiver go up my back.

At first the voices of the group were rather soft and gentle, but after Daddy Perfect appeared, people began to shout and clap their hands and jump up and down in time to the music. Another couple of spotlights illuminated the entire center of the stage. The rest of the Perfect Family was sitting behind Daddy Perfect. Four Perfect Sisters and Brothers were kneeling on either side of Daddy Perfect.

Daddy Perfect nodded to the kneeling Perfects who began crawling backwards to the edge of the stage where they lowered themselves over the side. The overhead lights went on. The audience was in a frenzy. Jane had nudged me, and I began jumping up and down and clapping my hands and pretending to chant. I couldn't understand a word of what people were singing. Tears of joy were running down the faces of a number of the chanters. They were really having fun.

Daddy Perfect turned his back on the group, strode to his tall thronelike chair and sat down. He raised one hand in the air. The chanting stopped immediately. This was a man who controlled an entire roomful of people—completely.

Maybe I was just a crazy kid like Jane had said. Maybe I would be stuck here with Myra forever. Then Jane leaned toward me.

"This is such a crock." And then she began giggling. Jane clapped her hand over her mouth to muffle the sound, an unnecessary gesture since the people around us had become mesmerized by the performance.

Performance. What was going on in front of us was a performance—and a very convincing one. But the smiling people around me thought they were seeing some kind of religious miracle. Daddy Perfect was smart. He was very good at what he did.

Daddy Perfect was a mighty foe, but I was a Holmes. I could see through the sham and fakery. I concentrated my Holmes powers on a plan to rescue Myra from this monster. When Daddy Perfect had raised his arms, I had noticed a rip under his armpit. An omen. A sign. I had seen an imperfection—a split in the Perfect seam of things. Suddenly I knew what I would have to do to rescue Myra.

# 27

"HAIL DADDY," shouted a voice from the congregation.

"HAIL DADDY!" the people responded.

"PRAISE MOMMY!" yelled another voice.

"PRAISE MOMMY!" shrieked everyone.

"SILENCE," blared a voice over the public-address system.

There was silence.

Immediately, Mommy Perfect rose from her throne. The Perfect kids, Sonny I and II, who seemed to be about sixteen or seventeen years old and who had been sitting ramrod straight, hands folded in their laps, began fidgeting as soon as Mommy's back was to them. One began chewing on his nails. The other slipped a magazine from under his robe and began reading it. Daddy Perfect ignored them.

Mommy Perfect glided to a microphone at the front of the stage. "Children of the Garden, former filth of the world, followers of our Perfect Master, let us proceed with the Punishment of Purity."

"Punishment of Purity?" I whispered to Jane as most of the people slid down in their seats. Some hid their faces behind their hands. Many groaned.

Jane didn't answer me. She had also slumped over and was trying to become invisible.

"The list, please," demanded Mommy Perfect, holding out a hand. A handmaiden tiptoed onto the stage and held out a sheet of paper. Mommy snatched it from her and began reading names. They were in alphabetical order, and each time she moved onto a new letter, a few people straightened in their seats.

"Forward Dirty Souls," Mommy said, when she was through reading. Ten people got up and shuffled to the front of the room. They stood beneath the stage in a clump and looked up at Mommy Perfect.

Then, one by one, Mommy called them up onto the stage. Each kneeled in front of her. Each was scolded and insulted. Each seemed to deflate and wilt under the abuse. In the end, Mommy placed her hand on the head of each drooping person and said, "Mommy forgives you. You are cleansed."

Each newly cleaned person gave Mommy a big smile, thanked her a number of times and crawled backwards off the stage. This entire procedure took about three minutes per Dirty Soul. It really moved along. There were only two people left—a man and a woman. I could tell from their outfits that they were high up in the cult. Mommy Perfect crumbled the sheet of paper and tossed it aside.

"Those whom Mommy has just graciously cleansed through the Power of Punishment are back on the Path to Perfection. Mommy will not waste her time helping these two backsliding ingrates. Banish the Brother. He will be shunned for an entire week and live in the kennels with the dogs. As for this Sister of Treachery, this Speck of Foulness, this Slimy Spiritual Polluter, this FORMER Perfect, Premium Grade . . ." Mommy Perfect paused to let that sink in. The congregation gasped. The former Sister Perfect, Premium Grade, collapsed on the floor, weeping.

"Take her away," ordered Mommy Perfect. "From this moment on, she is once again an IMP. Tonight, all her possessions will be packed and donated to the closest Nearly Perfect Shoppe, and as of tomorrow, she will move into the IMP quarters."

The guards dragged the sobbing sister out of the hall. For a long time, we could hear her screaming, "Mommy, please forgive me. I'll be good. Don't demote me. I'm sorry."

"That was awful." I felt sympathy for the poor woman.

"Demotions are like death to the Perfectionists," whispered Jane. "Any of them would rather be thrown in jail for a year than lose their rank."

"I figured that out for myself," I answered.

"Sure you did, Holmes."

"You just don't understand how astute I am despite my years," I said.

"I'll believe it when I see it," said Jane.

"See what?" I asked.

"See this place from the other side of the fence, Detective Holmes."

"Stop using my real name," I hissed into her ear.

"Shhhhhh!" said Jane. Daddy Perfect had gotten up. About

five spotlights went on at once—making him so bright that he almost glowed.

"Wow," I said. "It's a wonder he isn't blinded by all that light."

"Shhhhhhh," said Jane again, and then added, "Dark contact lenses."

"My children, Daddy Perfect greets you with a message from beyond." Daddy spoke with his arms raised and head thrown back.

"OOhhhhhhh," said the Children of Perfection.

"The message is . . ." But before Daddy Perfect could finish his sentence, the lights went out. The microphone went dead. There was instant pandemonium.

"Keep calm! Don't panic! It's just an electrical failure!" People were shouting orders over the noise of the milling, nervous congregation.

Jane grabbed onto my arm. "One too many lighting effects." She giggled.

"Maybe," I said. "And maybe something else happened."

"What?" hollered Jane. The din was getting louder and louder.

"Can't say, exactly. It's my Holmes instincts at work."

"Bull," said Jane.

Before I could answer, there was the noise of gunshots. Jane and I hit the floor.

"Stop shooting, you idiot. STOP SHOOTING!" Daddy Perfect's voice could be heard over everything. "SHUT UP, ALL OF YOU," he went on. "SHUT UP!"

The lights went on—first the stage lights and then the houselights. Some people were lying on the floor, heads covered with their hands. Others had made it to the doors and were about to run into the night. Jane and I, seeing Daddy Perfect clutching an armed guard by the back of his neck, returned to our seats.

"GET BACK TO YOUR PLACES," shouted Daddy Perfect. "Nothing's wrong." He waved away the armed guards who had apparently jumped onto the stage to surround the Perfect Family when the lights went out. He gave the guard he was holding a kick in the rump and grabbed his rifle away from him.

Once again, Daddy Perfect stood alone. He tossed the rifle onto the floor and raised his arms above his head. The houselights were extinguished. Making no mention of what had just taken place, Daddy Perfect began speaking exactly where he had left off before the blackout.

# 28

"Today's message from the Almighty came to me while I was standing in the Perfect Pumpkin Patch. BEHOLD THE PUMPKIN and rejoice!" boomed Daddy Perfect.

As Daddy Perfect spoke, a curtain at the back of the stage parted. Behind it was a glass wall. The stage went dark, and the hill behind the building shone from the light of maybe twenty high-powered spotlights. On top of the hill, growing on the very edge of the precipice, was the largest pumpkin I had ever seen in my life.

"The Pumpkin of Perfection," Daddy intoned.

"The Pumpkin of Perfection," the Children of Perfection whispered in awe.

"Daddy Perfect's Pumpkin," Daddy Perfect said.

"Daddy Perfect's Pumpkin," they all said.

"The message is that it is ready. IT IS READY! Our constant vigil has produced a Perfect Vegetable, a Perfect Prizewinning Vegetable. Today we weighed our Perfect Pumpkin,

and it will win the prize. It is the largest Pumpkin of all time
—600 pounds."

"Ahhhhh," said Daddy Perfect's followers.

"What is this all about?" I whispered to Jane.

"Daddy is entering that thing in a national contest. There's
a two-thousand-dollar prize for the heaviest pumpkin," answered Jane.

"But what does this have to do with the cult?" I asked.

"He had round-the-clock crews watering and feeding and
weeding the pumpkin patch. Daddy Perfect likes to win con-
tests. It's his thing. He also doesn't mind the prize money."

The curtains closed, and the Perfect Pumpkin was hidden
from sight. Daddy Perfect, once again illuminated by the
stage lights, was smiling.

"Now get ready for the exercise. Are you ready to share a
few moments of Bliss with your Daddy Perfect?"

"Yes," shouted the group. We were all on our feet, carrying
benches and chairs to the sides of the room.

"What about the message from beyond?" I asked Jane.

"That was it."

"What was it? The thing about the Pumpkin being ready
—that was the message?"

"Sure."

"What kind of message from the Almighty is that?" I asked
while helping Jane stack a bench on top of another bench.

"Sometimes they're better. Sometimes not. Now be quiet
and enjoy." Jane winked at me.

The entire cult had formed a huge U-shaped line. The open
end of the U was facing the wall opposite the stage.

"Prepare yourselves to behold Perfection." Daddy's voice
seemed to be coming from everywhere—the floor, the walls,
the ceiling. I deduced that additional speakers must have been
turned on. The entire huge meeting hall was specially wired
for sound.

"Now gaze upon Perfection!"

The back wall parted in the middle, and the two halves slid aside. When the overhead lights went on, I realized that we had been moving around in semidarkness. Our eyes had simply adjusted to the low light. The normal light seemed brilliant.

"The man could get an Oscar for special effects," I mumbled.

"You ain't seen nothin' yet," Jane said, giggling.

Spotlights lit up the empty doorway. No one seemed to be breathing. Into the ring of light moved a shining, golden and white object. Breath was let out in a big group sigh.

"BEHOLD!" said Daddy Perfect. "The Phantom of Perfection."

The largest, whitest, most polished, most perfect Rolls-Royce convertible limousine was pushed slowly into the center of the Temple of Perfection meeting hall. It was so bright, it hurt my eyes. I had to blink a few times before I could focus on it. I squinted, and it looked as if the door handles, the grill, the bumpers, the hubcaps and all the metal trim were made of gold.

"Gold?" I said.

"Gold," Jane answered.

Daddy Perfect started talking again. I stared at the Phantom of Perfection. Jane stared at the Phantom of Perfection. Everyone stared at the Phantom of Perfection.

This is ridiculous, I thought, just before I felt myself beginning to relax in a very strange way.

# 29

Beams of light bounced off the Phantom of Perfection. After a minute or so, the remainder of the meeting hall went dark. I told myself it was an illusion, but I felt as if I were floating in space—a satellite of the shining car. All I could see was its brightness. All I could hear was Daddy Perfect's voice. He was talking in a gentle, soothing way. He was talking to me.

"Rest, child, rest. Let yourself drift into the Perfect Emptiness. All you can hear is your Daddy's voice. All you can see is the light of the Phantom. It is leading you deep, deep into sleep. It is showing you the way to Perfection. Sleep, sleep."

Then Daddy Perfect began to count slowly. "Ten. You are going deeper and deeper into a happy sleep. Nine. Let yourself follow my voice. Relax. Eight. . . ."

I was so relaxed. My knees were beginning to buckle. I felt myself sinking toward the floor. I was drifting on a green lake. A cool breeze was blowing. In the distance, I could see a stairway leading up to a bright golden heaven. Where was I?

WHERE WAS I? My sharp Holmes sixth sense shrieked inside my head. You are being hypnotized. YOU ARE BEING HYPNOTIZED!

"Wait a second!" I said out loud. "I am being hypnotized!" I pinched myself, hard. I was groggy. I pinched myself again. My head cleared. I opened my eyes. I looked around. Some people were swaying back and forth. Some were sitting on the floor slumped over. All had their eyes closed. Next to me Jane was standing, head drooping onto her chest, arms hanging limply at her sides.

"Jane, wake up," I whispered. I reached over and poked her. No response.

I closed my eyes and swayed in her direction. When I got as close as I could to her head, I whispered again, "Jane, wake up. Wake up." On the next sway, I pinched her viciously.

"Yipes!" Jane squealed and opened her eyes. "Why did you do that?"

"You were being hypnotized," I whispered.

"No, I wasn't," she insisted. "I was just pretending. DP hasn't been able to get to me for weeks."

"Then why didn't you answer me when I spoke to you?"

"Because I wanted to see what you would do."

"Why didn't you warn me about this if you knew that Daddy Perfect was going to hypnotize everyone?" I was very angry.

"I wanted to see if you could figure it out for yourself."

"Thanks a whole lot, Jane. I think that was very hostile of you."

"Don't be mad. I would have awakened you before he got started on the other junk."

"What other junk?"

"Shhhh. Any minute now. Better shut up before he realizes we're not in his power." Jane sank to the floor and slumped over. I joined her.

"You are now in a deep sleep," cooed Daddy Perfect. "Life in the Garden of Perfection is Perfect. You LOVE your Daddy Perfect. You LOVE your Mommy Perfect. You are happy. You feel like smiling all of the time. You love your Daddy so much that anything he asks you to do you will do." Daddy Perfect was talking in a sleazy voice.

I peeked at the Perfectionists. They were all zonked out. The only people who were still upright were the Perfects, who were now walking slowly around the circle of followers. Mommy Perfect bent over and poked about every fifth person with one of her long, dangerous-looking red nails.

"The marks are out like lights," she said. "Your father is a real master, Sonny. Isn't he?"

"Yes, Mommy," answered both Perfect sons, who were walking behind their parents.

"Test that one. It's important," said Daddy Perfect. I had my eyes closed, but I could hear them all approaching. I braced myself.

I felt a sharp, knifelike object dig into my back. I forced myself to stay absolutely still.

"She's asleep. Were you worried?"

"No, of course not. But with that much money at stake, why take chances?"

"Children." Daddy Perfect raised his voice. "Children of the Garden, when I say so, you will awaken refreshed. You will feel WONDERFUL. You will be filled with happy contentment. You will love your Daddy and Mommy Perfect more than ever. WAKE UP! WAKE UP! Open your eyes and wake up!"

I opened my eyes. All around me, people were waking up. They were all smiling. I smiled too.

"Children," said Daddy Perfect, "did you all experience Bliss?"

"Oh yes, Daddy, yes," everyone answered. Many of them sighed. Several brushed tears from their eyes.

"Then thank your Daddy properly," said Daddy.

"Thank you, Daddy dear, thank you, Daddy dear, thank you, Daddy dear." The cultists began chanting and clapping their hands and dancing up and down. Using the din as cover, I spoke to Jane out of the side of my mouth.

"What is Bliss?" I asked.

"What they all just experienced. The hypnotism."

"They call it Bliss?"

"They don't realize what it is. They never remember what he actually says. All they know is that when they wake up, they feel happy and they love the Perfects more than ever."

"How long do those feelings last?"

"I'm not sure, but Daddy Perfect rarely lets more than three days go by before providing them with more Bliss."

"Mommy Perfect called everyone marks," I said.

"She always does when we're supposed to be under his spell. Do you know what it means?"

"Sure," I said.

"Well, what?"

"A mark is someone you mean to swindle. It's an old confidence-man word. It is also used by carnival people to describe customers who play the games of chance."

"You know a whole lot for a kid."

"I'm a Holmes, a detective. I make it my business to know things."

"I'm impressed."

"Thank you."

"You're welcome."

I was getting tired. While we spoke, Jane and I had been clapping our hands and jumping up and down with the rest of the Children of Perfection so we wouldn't look suspicious.

The noise of the chanting was subsiding. Mommy Perfect had climbed into the Perfect limousine. Two handmaidens stepped forward and held out two white jumpsuits. A third placed a white rug on the floor near the car. First one son and then the other stepped onto the rug, was dressed in a jumpsuit and stepped into the car.

"What is that all about?" I whispered.

"Cleanliness. The Perfectmobile lives in a padded, velvet-lined garage. The kids are not allowed in it unless they are covered up. Mommy can't stand the idea of dirt getting on her upholstery or carpeting."

"I'm surrounded by lunatics," I said.

"You're telling me?"

"Now Mommy Perfect will show you more proof that we

are smiled upon by God," Daddy Perfect's voice boomed. "Look, children, look!"

Mommy Perfect lifted up a white leather portfolio. She flipped it open and held it for all to see. There must have been twenty blue first-place prize ribbons displayed in front of us.

"Ohhhhhhhhhhhh," said everyone.

"You see, Children on the Path. YOU SEE!" Daddy Perfect was revving up again. "Mommy Perfect's Perfect Phantom Rolls-Royce limousine—the world's purest object—the world's CLEANEST object—the world's WHITEST object —has been Blessed from Above. It has won EVERY competition it has been entered in. What you see before you is the Queen of Cleanliness sitting in a MIRACLE!

"This car is so pure, that if Mommy Perfect wished, she could drive it straight to Heaven! Tomorrow we shall wrap the Shining Wonder in plastic and transport it to its final show. After that, Mommy has decided to have the Phantom of Perfection encased in a block of Lucite and put on display for the world to see. But, Children of the Garden—Little Beloved Perfectionists—tonight the Imperfects will get the chance to participate in the FINAL POLISH OF PERFECTION!"

"YAAAAAAAAAAAAAY!" shouted the Imperfects. I felt Mommy's eyes on me. "Yaaaaaaaay!" I shouted.

"Imperfects step forward!" All the Imperfects formed a tight ring around the car. The rest of the Brotherhood sat down on the floor. The Imperfects were handed white, seamless cotton gloves, which we all put on.

"COMMENCE POLISHING," Daddy ordered.

I joined right in as the Imperfects began rubbing the Phantom of Perfection. As far as I could tell, there wasn't a finger mark or a speck of dust on it before we began. We rubbed the fenders. We rubbed the hood. We rubbed the gold-plated trim, the gold hubcaps, the perfectly clean white rubber tires.

111

While we polished the gleaming automobile, a handmaiden, wearing white overalls and white cloth boots over her shoes, got into the front seat of the Perfectmobile and buffed the white glove-leather upholstery.

My arms began to feel as if they were filled with lead. I had to concentrate very hard to keep them moving. I noticed that all the Imperfects seemed to be in pain—their smiles and expressions of contentment had been replaced by grimaces.

"Finish!" Mommy Perfect was standing in the car. At her command, all Imperfect arms stopped moving.

"Back. Away!" she called out.

We all backed away from the car. Mommy Perfect opened the door, stepped down and, without so much as a glance at the result of our hard work, marched toward the stage. The crowd parted. The Perfect kids removed their coveralls and followed their mother. As the second Perfect kid passed us, he winked at Jane and stopped for a moment.

"Hi Jane," he whispered.

"Hi Pete, how goes it?" she answered. Jane's face had gotten a soft, dreamy look on it. The Perfect kid had a goofy expression to match. I deduced that they liked each other—a whole lot.

"Cruddy as usual. Want to go to a movie?" Pete made kind of a snorting noise.

"Sure, Pete, anytime." Jane smiled.

"SONNY II, WHAT ARE YOU DOING?" Mommy Perfect's sharp voice was like a slap. Pete flinched and answered.

"Coming, Mommy Dearest!" Pete winked again at Jane and left.

"Sonny II?" I asked.

"She calls them Sonny Perfect I and Sonny Perfect II. Actually his name is Pete and his brother's is Anthony." Jane looked sad.

"Do you like him, Jane?" I asked.

"I guess. What does it matter? We're both prisoners here."

"Bedtime, IMPs. Follow me!" Clara had appeared. The female IMPs formed a line and marched back to the barracks.

"Ten o'clock and all is well," said Clara as she flipped the light switch.

I lay on my bed. I had exactly two hours to accomplish the most important part of the rescue and escape—getting my hands on Myra. I allowed myself one satisfying thought before I put my mind to work on the problem.

"My sister is a jerk!" I whispered to the darkness.

"Amen to that," said Jane.

# 30

In the darkness, I listened to the IMPs for about fifteen minutes. The occasional cough, the twisting and turning in bed, the fluffing of pillows finally stopped. All I could hear was steady breathing and quiet snoring. They were asleep.

I pushed back my blanket and eased my legs over the side of my cot. I pulled on my coveralls and picked up my shoes. I was about to get up when a dark shape—darker than the darkness of the room—loomed in front of me. Before I could respond, a cold and clammy hand covered my mouth.

I tried prying the awful hand off my face while I struggled to get away. I couldn't.

"Easy, Niece," a voice breathed in my ear. "It's Irene. Nod your head if you understand."

I nodded. Irene released me. "Let's get out of here," I whispered and headed for the door. A hand grabbed my arm.

"Let go, Irene," I hissed.

"Who's Irene? It's me—Jane."

"I thought you were asleep."

"How could I sleep with you dropping hints about getting out of here? I'm going with you."

"Get dressed," I said.

"I never undressed. Who's Irene?"

"Shhhh. Let's get moving." I tiptoed toward the door. I had the knob in my hand.

"Hold it right there!" someone rasped.

"Oh no," moaned Jane.

"Who goes there?" demanded Irene.

"What do you want, Clara?" I asked, figuring out who belonged to the strange, hoarse whisper.

"Gotcha!" whispered Irene, who had leaped behind Clara and had pinned her in a hammerlock.

"Urrgh," said Clara, dropping what appeared to be five stuffed shopping bags.

"Let her go, Irene, she's a senior citizen."

"Am not," said Clara, rubbing her neck.

"Sorry, ma'am," apologized Irene.

"Don't call me ma'am, it makes me sound old," groused Clara.

"Shut up!" I demanded. "Follow me!" I walked into Clara's little room. They squeezed in after me.

"What are you all doing here?" I asked.

"Came to see if you needed help, Niece."

"I want to leave here with you and go back to school."

"The call of the wild has gotten to me again. I want to wander, to be free to roam the world, to—"

"OK, OK," I interrupted. I turned to Irene.

"Why aren't you at the command post? It's my case. What if I telephoned you and you were wandering around in the night?" And then I noticed what Irene was wearing. "And why are you wearing a wet suit, rubber gloves and flippers, Irene?"

114

"Why is she carrying five shopping bags filled with junk?" asked Irene, pointing to Clara.

"This is not junk. These are my worldly possessions. I am a shopping-bag lady. I am required by code to carry these bags with me whenever I travel."

Jane had begun to whimper and giggle at the same time. She was getting hysterical.

"Irene, the wet suit?" I asked.

"The fence," she answered.

"The fence?"

"Protection."

"From the electricity?"

"Elementary, Niece."

"Naturally. A simple deduction. I suppose it worked, since you're here. How did you climb the fence with flippers on?"

"With difficulty."

"Why did you choose them?"

"Only rubber shoes I could find on short notice."

"Why are you still wearing them?"

"Neglected to bring another pair of foot gear along."

"Here," offered Clara, who had been following our exchange carefully. She held out a ratty old pair of smelly sneakers. Irene took them without comment and kicked off her flippers. They fit.

"One more question, Irene. Did you short out the electric fence when you climbed over it?"

"Yes. All the lights in the place went out. Unfortunately, they managed to repair the power supply before I could cut the fence."

"Too bad," I said. "However, I have a plan which does not include the electric fence. You can all come along, but we have to move fast. Clara, you can't take all those bags with you. I'm sorry."

"These are my things. They go where I go. I told you, I am a shopping-bag lady."

"Right now, you are an escaping prisoner of war. Escaping prisoners do NOT carry all their worldly goods with them," chimed in Irene.

"War?" said Clara.

"Whatever," replied Irene.

"Look, I'm going. I'm on a schedule." I eased open the door to Clara's room and moved to the outer door. In a moment, I was in the open air. As I knew they would be, my three companions were right behind me.

"Stick to the shadows, stay low and don't make any noise," I whispered.

"OK."

"Right-o."

"Good idea," they all answered.

"Shhhhh," I said.

"GRRRRRKKKKK." Something squawked loudly.

Three of us dove for the side of the building. Clara put down her shopping bags and calmly rummaged around inside one of them.

"Clara, get over here. There's something out there," I said.

"No, there isn't. That was Samson. I'm just checking to see if he's all right."

"Who's Samson?" I asked as we suspiciously moved out of the shadow.

"My parakeet," said Clara.

"He's in the shopping bag?" I envisioned a poor squashed little bird smothered under Clara's sweaters and underwear.

"His cage is in here. He just woke up from being jostled and was surprised. He'll be fine now."

"Let's go!" I ordered and moved quickly toward my destination.

116

# 31

We moved from the darkness of the woods to the darkness of the shadow behind a dormitory. From there I led our small band of escapees toward a clump of large trees. The bright spotlights had been dimmed quite a bit—probably an economy measure since most of the TOP members seemed to have gone to bed. Nevertheless, it was light enough for us to find our way easily and therefore light enough for someone to spot us. And it was deadly quiet.

We crept over lawns and paths and driveways. We skulked in any shadow we could find. We moved from tree to tree in single file—a little snakelike group winding its way up the hill. We had gotten about two hundred feet from our starting point and were resting in the shadow of a small building when the silence of the night was broken by a horrible, roaring, animal scream. Through the air flew four legs, lots of fur and more teeth than I had ever remembered seeing. It was headed for a throat—any throat. It didn't seem particular.

Being first in line, it occurred to me that I was about to experience mutilation and pain. I threw my arms up to protect my face as I turned to shove the others out of the way. I had forgotten completely about the vicious, patrolling guard dogs. We were about to be torn into pieces, and it would be all my fault. I felt terrible.

"Now, now, you stop that this minute, King. You be a good boy, and Clara will give you a treat." King's teeth disappeared back into his mouth the second he heard Clara's voice. He landed about six inches from me, sat down and began wagging his tail and panting.

"What a good boy, King," said Clara and then she made some sounds in a high-pitched voice that sounded like *"weee-deee, weeedeee, weeedeee, weeeeedeeeee."*

Upon hearing them, King went out of his mind with pleasure. He flopped on the ground and rolled on his back, waving his feet in the air. Clara scratched his belly and told him he was her good baby. Then she offered him a handful of food —which appeared to be parakeet seed, but it was pretty dark, so I won't swear to that. Whatever it was, King ate it, licked Clara's hand and leaned against her leg.

"These are my friends, Kingie boy. You come with us and be quiet." Clara picked up her shopping bags as if nothing unusual had happened. "It's OK to go now. King and I are old friends. We've taken many a walk at night around here when I couldn't sleep. Kingie hates belonging to the Temple. He wants to escape with us."

"Oh," I said. There wasn't time to argue the point or to ask how Clara and an apparently trained killer guard dog had become friends. I wondered how Clara knew King's opinion of his home. However, not wanting to waste time or face all those teeth again, I let King fall in line behind Clara. We resumed our stealthy sneaking.

Actually, with King on our side bringing up the rear, I felt a little safer. Then it happened. Out of the darkness came another beastly, screaming roar.

"Don't know this one personally. You're on your own," said Clara as the furry, toothed monster left the ground.

Irene pushed in front of me. "Never fear, Niece. I have an old Tibetan trick or two up my sleeve."

Holding her hand straight out in front of her like a policeman stopping traffic, Irene said, "Peace, brother dog."

We're goners, I thought to myself.

For the second time in a matter of minutes, we were facing deadly peril, but nobody screamed. In fact, I think we all stopped breathing while we waited for death to strike. Then the most astonishing thing happened. The beast actually stopped its charge mid-leap and dropped to the ground. Teeth sparkling in the night, it crouched, stared at Irene and growled.

Irene talked to the dog. I had the impression that she was shouting because her voice seemed to bypass the ears and enter directly into the brain. In reality, Irene spoke in a strange whisper and somehow took control of the dog's mind. The dog stopped growling. It stopped snarling. Its flattened ears stood up. Its tail began to wag.

This is what Irene said: "Violence is wrong, dog friend. Violence is what the bad humans have taught you. It is against your gentle nature. You have been deceived. You are now free to throw off the chains of oppression. You are no longer obligated to destroy your soul by doing the dirty work of unworthy blackguards. My friend, I accept you into my pack. Come, be peaceful with us. Peace."

There is no proof that the dog understood a single word Irene said to it. To this day, I believe that HOW Irene communicated had more effect than exactly WHAT she communicated—but I'll never really be sure. All I know is that in the approximately sixty seconds it took for Irene to slowly say what she said, the dog changed from a miserable, dangerous guard dog into a sweet, puppylike, friendly pet.

"I think this is the one they call Lucrezia Borgia," said Clara, scratching the now gentled dog behind the ears.

"She'll need a new name when we get out of here," answered Irene, "something which will reflect her true nature. Isn't that right, girl?" Lucrezia Borgia wagged her tail.

Once again we moved out of the shadows and headed through the light toward the next spot of darkness. Lucrezia Borgia fell in behind King. Irene had moved up and was just behind me. After this last experience, I was glad for her company and strange abilities.

The vicious guard dogs had been trained to patrol specific

parts of the Temple of Perfection property. I deduced that each time we crossed into a new territory, we were attacked by its dog protector. Unfortunately, there was no way for us to tell when this was about to happen. Clara was no help in the matter because she had always taken her walks with King in a very small area near the dormitory—King's own territory. She had only seen the other dogs when they were penned up in the kennel during the day.

We crossed into new dog territory two more times before reaching our first destination. We knew we had done so because, upon setting foot over the invisible line, we were attacked. Irene had the opportunity to demonstrate that taming Lucrezia Borgia was no fluke.

Our chances of getting caught were increasing rapidly. Not only were we closer to the center of things, but it was starting to take quite a while for our expanded band to move from shadow to shadow without being spotted. Being the leader, I went first. I was followed by Irene, Jane, Clara, King, Lucrezia Borgia, Prince and Godzilla. Our escape was turning into a parade.

In addition, Clara refused to leave any of her shopping bags. She also refused to allow anyone to help her carry them. Each time it was Clara's turn to race from one dark place to the next, there would be a whole lot of rustling and banging and rattling as the bags crashed into each other and their contents—which turned out to be mostly things other than clothing—bounced around. There would also be a great deal of squawking and mumbling, because Samson the parakeet did not like being flung about inside a dark bag.

At one point, I remarked that I always thought birds slept at night. Clara's reply was, "Not during escapes."

"If we get out of here without getting caught, it's going to be a miracle," whispered Jane while we waited for Godzilla to make his dash through the light.

"Nonsense," said Irene. "My young relative, Sherelee

Holmes, is brilliant. She is leading an excellent escape. We must all express confidence in her leadership qualities and in her razor-sharp intellect. I, for one, feel safe in Sherelee's able hands.

"By the way, Niece, when and how do you intend to get your sister?"

"Right now, Irene, right now." We had reached the darkened meeting hall. "Does anyone have a watch?" I asked.

"It's ten minutes to midnight," said Irene.

"Perfect. Follow me, everyone." I raced through the side door of the hall. It was pitch-black inside.

"What now?" asked Irene.

"We disperse and wait. Jane, how many guards escort prisoners to pot-scrubbing duty?"

"I told you, one per prisoner."

"Just checking." I positioned my band of escapees for the ambush and gave them instructions.

Just as the dogs got into place, the door was pushed open, a hand reached in and flipped a switch and the overhead lights went on. Myra stumbled into the meeting hall. Brother Rodney was close on her heels.

"I hate getting up in the middle of the night to escort prisoners, so get a move on it," Rodney ordered, pushing Myra so she stumbled again.

"Get your hands off me, nerd. I won't wash any yicky, filthy pots and pans."

"Yes you will, Little Sister," Rodney sneered, "or you'll spend the rest of your life in jail."

They were about ten feet into the meeting hall when Irene and the dogs leaped at Rodney, Clara flipped the light switch off, and Jane and I grabbed Myra.

"HELP!" Myra screamed.

I put my hand over her mouth. "Shut up, Myra, it's me, Sherelee." Myra bit my thumb.

"Ouch. Why did you do that, you jerk? We're here to rescue

you." Despite the pain, I kept my hand in place. Myra was struggling and trying to scream.

"Cut it out, Myra, or we'll all be caught." Myra didn't seem to hear me. She elbowed me in the stomach and kicked Jane in the shin.

"Can't we hit her over the head or something?" gasped Jane, who was trying to keep Myra's arms pinned to her sides.

"I wish," I said, "but she is my sister."

"Trouble, Niece?" Irene had found us in the darkness.

"Myra won't cooperate." My thumb really hurt, and Myra was trying to take another bite out of my hand.

Irene shone a little flashlight in Myra's face, which was distorted with anger and fear.

"I'm sorry, Myra, but I have no choice," Irene spoke softly into Myra's ear.

Irene talked rapidly in a strange language for about thirty seconds. Myra began to relax. She stopped struggling. She stopped trying to destroy my hand. Irene flicked on the flashlight once more. Myra's face was peaceful, her eyes glazed.

"That should hold her for a while. That guard fellow is tied up and stuffed into a closet. What's next?" We were standing in darkness once more. I could hear the dogs panting. I could also hear voices approaching the building.

"Let's get out of here fast. Is there another door, Jane?" We were in extreme peril, about to be discovered.

"Through the kitchen," Jane answered. "I'll lead the way."

"Everyone hold hands," I ordered. We linked hands and felt our way through the darkness. Irene dragged Myra behind her, and Clara brought up the rear with her clanking shopping bags making their terrible racket. Just as we exited through the kitchen door, all the lights in the meeting hall went on.

"Will they miss Myra and Rodney?" I asked Jane.

"Depends upon who's in there."

122

I crept up to a window and peered over the sill. Mommy Perfect was sitting on a chair next to the Phantom of Perfection. Three Perfects—two men and a woman—were working on the car. One was scrubbing the tires with what looked like a toothbrush. One was polishing the windshield, and the third was vacuuming the carpeting.

Irene had moved next to me. "You don't have to travel the world to observe exotic and unusual behavior, do you, Niece?"

"Jane," I said. "It's Mommy Perfect and some Perfects working on the car. Will they notice Myra's absence?"

"No. MP doesn't keep track of daily details around here. What she might notice eventually are the dirty pots—but she'll just order demerits for the person responsible."

"Then let's move on."

"Good. Where are we going?" Irene asked.

"To find the exit. We may have to overpower some guards again."

"You have a specific exit in mind?" asked Irene.

"It's what I found out from Harry. There's a tunnel."

"I know that way out," chirped Clara.

"What?" I said.

"I know the tunnel—it's the back way out of here. And it's not guarded."

"Are you sure, Clara?"

"I said so, didn't I? No guards."

"Have you ever seen the tunnel?" I asked.

Clara had begun humming to herself, and I was afraid I was losing her attention just when I needed it most.

"Daddy Perfect's special personal escape tunnel. It leads right onto Route 1. Been through it a couple of times. Just for fun. Us loonies can go anywhere—do anything—and nobody ever looks us in the eye. It's kind of fun—like being the invisible woman." Clara giggled.

"Where is the entrance to the tunnel, Clara?" I asked.

"Up there." Clara pointed to the big house on top of the highest hill—the home of the Perfect Family.

"Exactly where up there?"

"Up there. In Daddy Perfect's office."

"Swell," said Jane. "That sinks us. I vote for charging some guards at a gate and taking our chances at being shot."

"No. We go for the tunnel. Exactly where does it let out, Clara?"

"On the road. Route 1. Don't you listen to me?"

"I do. Where EXACTLY on Route 1? It's important, Clara." I kept my voice calm and gentle.

"Who knows? I'm a stranger to these parts myself. The country confuses me—no traffic lights, no corners, no curbs. There are trees at the end of the tunnel. Then the road. Why does it matter anyway? Once we're there, we're free. And free is free, right? We can ask directions." Clara began mumbling to herself. She sat down on the ground and hugged King.

"We have to move out, folks," I said. "Follow me. Stay hidden. I know exactly what we are going to do." And, for once, I did. As Clara had babbled, my Holmes brain had conceived a masterful way to deal with these new obstacles. I was about to complete my plan of escape.

I stood straight and tall as I gave my commands. I wanted to look brave and inspirational. Actually I was petrified that something would go wrong. But I had to remember what Great-great-grandpa Sherlock said whenever he found himself in impossibly difficult situations: "He who does not feel fear is a fool!"

# 32

I slipped through the shadows along the driveway with Lucrezia Borgia at my side. The killer dog had taken a liking to me. Whenever I stopped, she nuzzled my hand and licked my sore thumb. She was more trustworthy than Myra when it came to fingers.

I could see the inner gate and the guard station ahead of me. There were two guards leaning against the little guardhouse. Their rifles were propped against a big rock. The guards were smoking cigarettes and talking. They were not paying close attention to their guard duties.

"Irene," I whispered, "do you know how to control these dogs?"

"In what way, Niece?" she asked.

"Can you make them help us capture the guards?"

"I can ask them if they will consent to helping us in this time of trouble. After all, they have foresworn their lives of violence."

I groaned. "Irene, can you or can't you get them to help?"

"Of course I can." Irene huffed off toward King, Prince and Godzilla. Lucrezia Borgia gave my thumb one last lick and followed her. Irene squatted down. The dogs sat facing her. They appeared to be having a conference. Finally, Irene came back and reported, "They all agree. What do you want us to do?"

I told Irene my plan. She explained it to the dogs. They moved off into the shadows. I counted slowly to 200, and then I stood up and walked toward the guardhouse. The guards were so busy talking that I had to clear my throat once and cough a couple of times before they noticed me and dove for their rifles.

"Halt!" barked one.

"Who goes there?" ordered the other.

I halted and answered. "It's me. My name is Cynthia Vanderbelt, and I just got here today. I'm lost." I tried to sound as pitiful and as helpless as possible.

The guards walked toward me. When they were sure I was just a kid, they lowered their rifles.

"How did you get by the dogs?" the first one demanded.

"What dogs?" I asked innocently. They looked confused.

"Did someone forget to let the dogs out tonight?"

"I thought I saw Prince patrolling just a while ago."

"Maybe something's wrong."

It was working. The guards were forgetting I was there.

"I think I had better call the Big House. This might mean trouble."

"It had better mean trouble, or we'll be in trouble for waking them up."

"Naw, MP is in the meeting hall."

"Maybe we should go and report to her directly about the dogs."

"Well . . ."

The conversation went on and on. I eased away from the guards as Irene and the dogs circled behind them. At a silent signal from her, the dogs leaped on the guards' backs—two to a man. As they hit the ground, Irene and I rushed in and grabbed the rifles. The guards had turned sheet white.

"No sound out of you, or they'll rip your throats out," I commanded.

"Well, actually," began Irene, "their new philosophy won't allow—"

"Irene," I interrupted, "with all due respect, please shut up."

126

"Right-o, Niece."

We marched the guards into some thick brush and tied them together with cord from one of Clara's shopping bags. Irene then touched each guard's head with both of her hands, and they went to sleep like exhausted babies.

"I learned that one from a hermit in Nepal. Remind me to teach it to you, it's perfect for beginners."

"OK, Irene. Thanks."

We entered the inner compound and closed the tall metal gate behind us.

"Does anyone see an electric switch on this side of the fence?" I asked.

"Is this it?" asked Clara, pointing to a metal box attached to a tree trunk.

It was. Checking to see that all of us were clear of the barrier, I pulled the switch down.

"That will keep them away from us for a while," I said.

"How did you know the switch would be on this side and not in the guardhouse?" asked Jane.

"Simple deducing," I answered.

"What about the people inside the house?" Irene looked steadily at me.

"I've taken care of that. Come with me." I ran up the driveway. Just before we reached the house, I turned toward Daddy Perfect's vegetable garden.

"Where are we going?" Jane asked.

"To create a diversion."

"I'm tired," said Clara. "I don't think I can go on. I'm an old lady, you know. All this running is no good for me."

"Sit down here, Clara. You can rest for a while. We have work to do." I sat the still-mesmerized Myra next to Clara.

We were on the edge of Daddy Perfect's Perfect Garden. It was lit by a number of fluorescent lights—each one trained on one plant—each plant bearing exactly one giant vegetable or fruit. There was an enormous tomato—supported by a hammocklike contraption so it wouldn't break from the vine or touch the ground. There was a cucumber the size of a watermelon and a watermelon the size of three watermelons. Sleeping soundly, back propped against an enormous zucchini, was the night vegetable tender and guard. Irene and the dogs swiftly overpowered him and had him tied and subdued in minutes.

"Why are we here?" Jane was looking worried.

"Because of that." I pointed to the giant pumpkin.

"Ahhhhh," said Irene.

"Am I missing something?" asked Jane.

"Of course," answered Irene. "Brilliant, Niece, brilliant."

"What? What's brilliant?" asked Jane.

"My plan," I said. "Come."

The pumpkin was perched on the very edge of the clifflike hill. Beneath it was the electric fence, several small buildings and the compound's road. The hill was covered with small bushes and rocks.

"Let's get it over with," I said. "Be ready to run for the house as soon as it's rolling."

"Rolling?" asked Jane.

"Rolling. It's my diversionary tactic."

"How much does that thing weigh?" Jane did not look enthusiastic.

"About 800 pounds or so," said Irene.

"How are the three of us going to push it?"

"We don't have to move it much." I tried to sound encouraging.

"Not to worry, our determination is our strength! Once I successfully propelled a half-ton boulder over the side of a precipice—in Tibet."

"Why?" I asked.

"Bandits. A narrow escape."

Irene leaned her back against the giant pumpkin and braced her feet on the ground. I positioned myself next to her. There wasn't enough room for Jane, so she leaned over us and placed the palms of her hands on the pumpkin.

"One, two, three, PUSH!" I grunted.

Jane groaned.

Irene groaned.

I groaned.

The pumpkin rocked. We pushed harder. It rocked again. We pushed harder. We could feel it beginning to turn, like a giant ball.

"One, two, three, push," I gasped. We gave one last, enormous push, and the pumpkin moved away from us. We landed on the ground—Jane on her stomach, and Irene and me on our rear ends. I turned just in time to see the giant orange monster teeter on the edge of the cliff and then disappear over the side.

"Bravo!" called Clara, applauding loudly.

"Shhhhh," said Jane.

"Doesn't matter now," I said and got to my feet. "Let's get to the house as fast as possible. Who's going to lead Myra?"

"I will. But before we go, you must see this, Niece. It's wonderful." Irene was standing at the cliff's edge watching the pumpkin tumble.

We joined her. The pumpkin was really gathering momentum. It was uprooting bushes and loosening rocks. By the time it reached the inner fence, its speed was such that it was simply a blur.

We cheered as the great orange vegetable did not split apart upon hitting the electric fence but rather cut a circular hole in it. The sparks shot fifty feet in the air. The lights in the garden and the house above it went out, but the compound light stayed on.

People were beginning to shout and run. Doors slammed.

We flattened ourselves on the ground as we heard people running from the Big House behind us and start down the driveway toward the commotion.

Daddy Perfect was shouting as he ran, "RAID! RAID! HOLD OFF THE INVADERS! MAN THE BATTLE-MENTS! WHERE IS MOMMY?"

The pumpkin mowed down a storage house, crashed through several decorative wooden fences and then, just as we were sure it would have to begin to slow its journey, it flew off one last small hill—like a fat ski jumper. All the lights in the lower compound were on, so we had a wonderful view of the pumpkin sailing just like a glorious orange balloon—up —up—spinning. And then, almost in slow motion, it fell toward earth.

At the same moment, the Perfectmobile, the Phantom of Perfection, the soon-to-be immortalized World's Cleanest Object, rounded the corner on its way to its velvet garage. Its tires were covered by cellophane wrap, and its perfectly buffed white glove-leather convertible top was up—to keep any dust from marring the perfect upholstery.

The pumpkin began flying just as the Phantom came into sight at the bottom of the hill. Fate, accident, justice—all coordinated the landing of the Perfect Pumpkin and the arrival of the Perfect Car. They met suddenly, noisily and, some might say, gloriously.

The merging of the two Perfect Projects was almost mystical. The pumpkin easily tore through the leather roof of the car and landed squarely in the middle of the huge backseat, where it finally split apart. About a million pumpkin seeds, covered with orange, sticky pumpkin juice and pulp, shot into the air, spilled onto the seat, soaked into the carpeting and covered Mommy Perfect's entire body—for she was driving the car.

She braked. The Phantom came to a sudden stop. People

rushed over—too late to stop the remaining stringy pulp, juice and seeds of the shattered vegetable from oozing out and entirely filling the backseat area of the car.

"An excellent cosmic joke," said Irene, laughing.

"The blob returns to Earth," said Jane, giggling.

"That's what I call a real squash," said Clara, cackling.

"Where am I?" moaned Myra.

"Time to go. This is our only chance."

I ran from the edge of the cliff toward the house. My happy band of escapees followed closely at my heels, Irene dragging the awakening Myra behind her.

# 33

One half of the enormous double front door was open. I stood aside and made sure all the escapees entered the house. I pushed shut the door and felt for a lock. It was pitch-black inside the entry hall.

"I can't see," said Jane.

"Nobody can see, it's dark in here," said Clara.

"I shall provide some light," said Irene, switching on her small flashlight.

"Shine it over here, Irene." I still hadn't found any sign of a locking mechanism.

Irene moved the light over the perfectly smooth doors. There was no lock. However, leaning against the wall was a long, thick, wooden board. On either side of the doors were metal brackets

"Ah hah!" I said.

"Just so," said Irene.

"What?" asked Jane.

"An old-fashioned bar bolt—the kind used in castles and forts," I explained, trying to lift the board. Irene rushed over to help me. Together we slipped the board across the doors and fitted it into the brackets. It held both doors tightly shut.

"It will take a battering ram to break that down," chirped Irene.

"They could always come through the windows," someone complained. I couldn't see the face, but I recognized the voice. Myra was awake.

"Myra, how are you feeling?" I asked.

"What do you think you're doing, Sherelee? Look at the mess you've gotten us all into, playing detective. I'm going to tell Mother and Father—"

"Shut up, Myra," we all said at once.

"Where is the tunnel, Clara?" I asked.

"I'm confused in the dark. It's in Daddy Perfect's office. Can't we turn on a light?" I could hear Clara's shopping bags rattling as she moved around the entry hall.

"There are no lights, you ditz." I could hear the nasty smirk in Myra's voice.

"I was in Daddy Perfect's office this morning," I said. "It's off to the left." I bumped into someone as I began moving.

"That was my toe, Sherelee. Can't you be careful?" Myra's unpleasant voice rang out in the marble hallway.

"Shhhh, you idiot!" whispered Clara. "You'll get us all caught."

"Don't call me an idiot." Myra's voice got louder.

"Irene, can't you do something about her?" I asked.

"Certainly, Niece." I heard Irene's sneakered feet squeak across the smooth floor.

"Don't touch me, whoever you are!" Myra sounded panicky.

"Will you be quiet, then?" asked Irene.

"Yes," whispered Myra.

"And I am your aunt, Irene Holmes, your father's sister and the great-granddaughter of Sherlock Holmes."

Myra groaned and whispered, "I don't know what you're so tense about anyway—everyone is down the hill looking at the squashed car."

"Squashed car?" A male voice echoed through the hall.

The dogs pushed their way past us. I could feel them forming a line in front of our little group. Before we could take any action, a hand-held light went on above us. On the stairs, halfway up, sat Sonny Perfect II.

"What are you doing here, Pete?" Jane asked.

"I live here. What are you doing here?"

"We don't have time for this," I said. "Any minute now, they are going to figure out that someone pushed that pumpkin and come up here after us."

"You pushed the pumpkin? Did it hit the car? My mother's car?" Sonny II began laughing. The light jiggled up and down as his body shook.

"Now!" said Irene. She and the dogs rushed up the stairs and swarmed all over Sonny II. He kept right on laughing.

"Hi, Lucrezia. Good boy, King. Hey, stop licking me, Godzilla."

Irene had grabbed the battery-operated lantern. The dogs were pinning Sonny to the steps, but he didn't seem to mind.

"I love these guys. Are you taking them along on your escape?" he asked.

"What's it to you?" answered Myra.

"Yes," I said. "And I'm sorry, but we're in a hurry. We're going to have to tie you up. Irene—"

"Clara, any more rope in your bags?" Irene asked.

"Wait. Why don't you just take me along? Jane can tell you, I hate it here. I've been running away since I was five, but they always found me and brought me back. Take me with you, and I'll help."

I couldn't rely on Jane's opinion of Sonny II because she had a crush on him. I had to trust my Holmes instinct.

"You're in, Sonny II. Show us the tunnel entrance."

"Please call me Pete. This way . . ."

Pete pushed the dogs away and ran down the stairs. In Daddy Perfect's office, Irene held the lantern, and Pete pressed his hands along a wall. A panel swung open. I closed the office door and locked it.

"Help me move this," I said, going over to Daddy Perfect's desk. We all shoved the heavy, mahogany desk in front of the door and piled an armchair on top of it. Then I had everyone drag two heavy file cabinets near the entryway to the tunnel.

"Where is the telephone, Pete?" I asked.

Pete pointed to a small table near the window. I dialed. The phone rang five times.

"Where were you?" I growled.

"Sherelee, is that you? I'm so relieved. George went to the store for a few minutes, and Irene disappeared from here hours ago. I'm all alone. I was thinking of calling my mother but—"

"Watson, be quiet. This is important. The minute George gets back, tell him to drive to Route 1—behind the Temple of Perfection compound. Tell him to keep driving back and forth slowly—for about one mile—until we appear. Got that, Watson?"

"Let me write it down, Sherelee," Watson was whining.

"There's no time, Watson. Memorize it. George. Car. Route 1. Temple of Perfection. One mile. Back and forth. Do you have it?"

"I think so. I'm very nervous. I hate staying in this big house alone. Can I come along with George, please, Sherelee?"

"Do what you want, Watson—only give him the message. It is absolutely urgent."

134

"Is Myra with you? Where are you calling from? Are you in trouble?"

"Good-bye, Watson."

"Good-bye, Sherelee."

"Now we can get out of here." I tried to sound calm, but I didn't like the idea of leaving such an important message with Watson.

Making sure everyone was out of the office and through the panel, I leaned over and slid open all the file drawers in the first cabinet. It tipped forward slightly. I grabbed the top as best I could and pulled with all my strength. Irene, seeing what I was doing, reached over to help me. Her rubber gloves provided the necessary traction. The file cabinet crashed to the floor, partially blocking the tunnel entrance. We worked on the second cabinet. It crashed onto the first.

"That will slow them down a little," I announced.

"I am impressed with your foresight." Irene patted me on the back.

I stepped into what appeared to be a small room behind the wall. Pete reached around me and touched the wall. The panel slid closed. An overhead light went on.

"Separate generator," said Pete.

The room was lined with shelves of food. There were two cots neatly made into beds and a radio, a television, a short-wave radio and a small refrigerator, a large freezer and a stove. The only things missing were a source of running water and a toilet.

"There's a simple bathroom just inside the tunnel," said Pete.

"What's this for?" I asked. "And where is the tunnel?"

"This is my mother and father's private hidey-hole—in case their enemies come after them. It's designed so they can disappear for months at a time."

"Enemies?" I asked.

"The police. The Feds, in particular." Pete was moving the cots away from the wall.

"Which branch of the federal government might be after your parents?" asked Irene.

"The Treasury Department, probably. Got it." Pete had been searching for something along the baseboard. The bottom of the wall swung back, revealing the entrance to the tunnel.

"Let's block the way into this room and be on our way." I began dragging heavy objects to the place where we had entered the room. In minutes, all the appliances and piles of canned goods were blocking the entry space.

I pushed everyone into the tunnel. As the panel slid shut, I heard pounding and yelling coming from the house. The Perfectionists had discovered our plan and were after us.

The lantern had started to flicker.

"Batteries are going," said Irene, lighting her little flashlight just as the lantern went out.

"Are there lights in the tunnel?" I asked.

"No," said Pete.

"Yes," said Clara.

"Which is it?" I demanded. Now we could all hear shouts and smashing. They had broken into the house and were working their way into the office.

"Yes," said Clara. "Mommy Perfect had them installed last month."

"No kidding. How do you know?" asked Pete.

"I know, that's all." Clara must have found a switch, because the entire tunnel was suddenly lit by bare bulbs strung along its length.

"This way," said Clara. "Duck when you reach here."

Twenty feet into the tunnel, its ceiling suddenly dropped. Even I had to walk slightly bent over. Only the dogs were comfortable.

136

"How long is the tunnel?" I asked.

"About a mile or two," answered Clara.

"No more than a quarter of a mile," answered Pete.

"I can't walk this way. My neck is starting to hurt," whined Myra.

"Look, everyone, we had better begin to move faster. Once they get into the tunnel, things might get a little rough. Irene, could you lead the way—kind of set the pace?"

"Yes, Niece. But shouldn't I stay behind with you and protect our rear flanks from the blackguards?"

"I can set a fast pace," said Pete. "Clara, may I please help you carry some of those shopping bags?"

"Thank you, Sonny, I wouldn't mind that a bit."

Pete grabbed most of Clara's bags and took off down the tunnel. Clara, Myra, Jane, King and Prince went with them.

"Are you thinking what I am thinking, Niece?" asked Irene.

"I'm thinking two things."

"Precisely. The first is that we should darken the tunnel behind us. Right?"

"Right."

"What exactly is the second thing?"

"Daddy Perfect is going to send people to head us off at the mouth of the tunnel as soon as he realizes where we went."

"Our Great-grandfather Holmes was very fond of saying that a bad thought is often arrived at through excellent reasoning. To be forewarned is to be forearmed."

"Let's break the light bulbs, Irene." I ran back to the bathroom entrance where I had seen some mops and brooms. I grabbed two. I could hear the Perfectionists screaming and making loud banging noises. They were dismantling the barricades. They would be in the secret room in a few minutes.

Irene sent the dogs down the tunnel. She had trouble with Lucrezia Borgia, who seemed to want to stay by my side. I had to order the beast away. We ran backwards, keeping alert for pursuers as we smashed the overhead light bulbs—darkening the tunnel as we went.

"We're moving too slow, Irene," I gasped.

"I know. They should be in the tunnel any second now."

"I wonder how long it really is."

"Not even a quarter of a mile. Feel the flow of fresh air?"

"I hope you are right, because I think we should abandon this backward running and get out of here."

"Good idea, Niece."

Irene and I turned around and began running as fast as we could. We heard a loud crash and the shouts of many men.

"Uh-oh," said Irene and, without stopping, she reached behind herself and grabbed my hand. We began to move at an incredible speed.

"What's happening to us?" I asked.

"Tibetan walking trick. Great for covering long distances very fast."

"But we're running, Irene."

"Same principle. Save your breath. We're almost there."

As she said that, we leaped out of the tunnel and landed in a bunch of bushes. Lucrezia Borgia, reaching the tunnel exit at the same exact moment, landed on top of us, panting and drooling.

# 34

"Almost safe," said Irene.

"Maybe." I could hear our enemies scrambling down the tunnel. "Where are the others?" I asked.

"Pssst, is that you, Sherelee?"

"Where are you, Jane?" I asked.

"Behind this tree. We all are. The light from the tunnel is very bright, and we've been hearing voices in the woods heading this way."

"They're coming through the tunnel, too. Irene, hand me your rubber gloves."

"Let me do the honors, please."

Irene ran back to the tunnel, reached up and yanked at the electric wire. Sparks flew, and the lights went out. There was no moon that night, and the countryside was so dark that we might as well have all been blindfolded. Irene, using her flashlight, found her way back to us.

"Where is the road, Clara?"

"That way," said Clara, pointing in some direction we could not see.

"No, that way," said Pete, probably pointing in another direction.

The voices in the tunnel behind us were getting closer. We could hear branches breaking and shouting as searchers moved through the woods on our right. That gave us a choice of two directions.

"Irene?" I asked.

"It's your case, Niece," she answered.

"Well, the road has to be close by, because a fleeing Perfect would want to be whisked away by car quickly. I've decided. Forward!" I ordered. "Hold hands and move as fast as possible. Irene, you lead the way with the light. I'll stay in the rear with the dogs to cover the retreat. Hear that, dogs?"

The dogs milled around me as the others moved away. We waited and listened. The voices were definitely closing in. I could now hear noise off to the left. I had made the right choice. They were trying to encircle us. Holding on to Lucrezia Borgia's collar, I stumbled in the direction of my friends. The dogs now surrounded me protectively, King lead-

139

ing the way, and Godzilla—who must have weighed 130 pounds—bringing up the rear.

Lucrezia Borgia dragged me up a small hill and then stopped. We were out of the trees.

"Irene?" I whispered into the night.

"Over here." I saw a flashlight blink on and off twice.

Hearing her voice, the dogs ran to greet her. I stepped forward and stumbled. My knees hit a hard surface. The road. We had reached Route 1. Now, if Watson had given George the message, we were free.

"I'll be there in a minute," I whispered.

"You'll be nowhere, Cynthia Vanderbelt. You're coming home with us!"

A viselike grip held my arm. In seconds, I was surrounded by Temple of Perfection guards, each carrying a rifle and a flashlight.

"Where are your companions, Little Sister?" I stared up into the eerily lit face of Brother Perfect Lawton, First Class.

"What companions?" I asked.

"The ones who helped you to escape."

"Escape? Escape? I was just taking a little walk and got lost," I said loudly. I hoped Irene was moving the rest of our group away from my captors.

"Found Miss Moneybags, Daddy. Meet us on Route 1." BP Lawton spoke into a walkie-talkie. "Your goose is cooked, IMP. You'll probably spend the next three years in the House of Repentance. Now, where are your accomplices? Who are they? How did they know who you were? Were you followed here? Give me the information, and things will go easier on you."

"What are you talking about, Brother Lawton?" I asked innocently. His hand squeezed my arm even tighter. I winced in pain.

If Watson messed things up, I thought, I will spend the best

140

years of my life in jail—and that, for sure, is a thoroughly cooked goose.

I tried to remember something encouraging said by Great-great-grandpa Sherlock those few times he found himself trapped in similar situations—but all that came to me was, "When one jumps out of the frying pan and into the fire, it is wise for one to be carrying a bucket full of water." I couldn't remember if Great-great-grandpa had said that or if I had read it in a fortune cookie.

Not knowing didn't seem to help my state of mind or being one single bit.

"How come Daddy Perfect is coming down here?" I asked.

"Now that we've found you, he wants to lead the search for the ones who destroyed his pumpkin. You're just lucky that Mommy Perfect is in a state of collapse about her car or she'd be arriving, too."

The guards, thinking me securely in tow, wandered away —halfheartedly searching for the rest of the escapees.

"So?" I asked, trying to keep BP Lawton distracted.

"So? So? Have you any idea of what Mommy Perfect would do to you if she thought you had anything to do with ruining her Phantom of Perfection?" BP Lawton began to sputter. He also loosened his grip on my arm. I whistled loudly and shook my head as if responding to his agitation.

"Right. It's beyond words." Despite what he claimed, BP Lawton began a long speech describing what Mommy Perfect did to people when she was really angry at them. I tried not to listen to the details.

I felt a cold nose and a soft muzzle in my hand. A tongue licked my sore thumb. I looked down to see a shadow fade back into the woods. Lucrezia Borgia had arrived. In the darkness, I could feel rather than see the other dogs waiting —motionless. They had heard my whistle.

I concentrated so I could hear around the noise of BP

Lawton's yammering. There it was. The roar of a distant automobile engine approaching very fast. Then, from the other direction, another engine. One of those cars was Daddy Perfect's car. The other might be George's.

Headlights appeared from both directions. Both cars looked enormous, bearing down on us. One slowed, pulled over to the side of the road, stopped and trained its headlights on us. The other slowed but didn't stop. When it was even with me and BP Lawton, whoever was driving stepped on the gas and screeched away from us at about 80 miles an hour.

"Stupid fool," said BP Lawton. Daddy Perfect had gotten out of his limousine and was walking toward us. The headlights lit up his strange hair just as the stage lights head.

"Any progress, Lawton?" asked Daddy Perfect.

"We have this one, and I'm sure the others are around here."

"Put her in my car, and let's finish up this search."

BP Lawton began dragging me toward Daddy Perfect's car. I dug in my heels. The huge car which had roared past had turned around up the road and was speeding back toward us. Just as it reached where Daddy Perfect's car was parked, its driver turned on the high-beam headlights and blasted the horn.

"Now, Lucrezia!" I shouted. Lucrezia Borgia leaped out of the woods and grabbed BP Lawton's wrist. He let go of my arm.

The mysterious limousine screeched to a stop.

"King, Godzilla, Prince!" I hollered. The terrible trio jumped into the middle of the group of guards, surprising and terrifying them. As they tried to get away from the killer dogs, the animals tripped them, ran circles around them and, using their powerful teeth, pulled the rifles out of their hands.

"Come!" I called to the dogs.

They whirled around and followed me. I dove headfirst

142

through the open door of George's limousine, which was filling up fast with people and animals and shopping bags. Irene, Clara, Pete and Jane were scrambling in from the other side. Lucrezia Borgia, King, Godzilla and Prince had jumped over my body and were settling in happily on top of everyone else. Myra managed to get in the front seat next to Watson.

We slammed the doors behind us and pushed down the locks.

"All in?" shouted George.

"All in!" I shouted back so he could hear me over the noise. George stepped on the gas and peeled away from the angry Perfectionists just as they began to surround the limousine and pound on it with their fists.

"Hey, little bloodhound," said George over his shoulder. "Nice going, little big eyes, nice going. You outwitted the small-time big shot. You flimflammed a flimflammer."

"Thanks, George," I said. "But I had a whole lot of help from my friends here."

"Real class." George's voice faded away as he concentrated on maneuvering the speeding limousine through the night.

"Do you think they'll follow us?" asked Jane.

"Not at this speed, dearie," answered Clara.

Myra and Watson, sitting in the uncrowded front seat with George, whined about how uncomfortable they were all the way back to the Vogel home. The rest of us settled in and took a very comforting and long overdue nap.

# 35

So that I wouldn't be grounded until I was eighteen years old, I decided not to mention any of my experiences with the Perfectionists to my parents. Of course I didn't have to worry about Myra giving me any credit at all for her return home. When we got home from the Vogels the next day, Myra went to our room and began complaining about how she no longer had any possessions.

Our parents, thrilled to see the prodigal child return from the evil world, took Myra shopping that very afternoon. I collected all the insignificant junk Myra had unloaded on me and piled it on her bed. When she found it there, she didn't even say thank you.

In about a week, my parents, in an effort to prove that there is no place like home, had provided Myra with an entire new wardrobe, a new typewriter, radio, stereo, camera and one very sleek, modern desk lamp. At least that was an improvement over the old ugly antique. Myra, as far as I could tell, was exactly the same Myra she had always been.

To this day, she has never mentioned her rescue from the Temple of Perfection. Except for a demand that I call her Sister Perfect Myra when in our room, she has never indicated that she remembers a single thing about her experience. Naturally Myra has never thanked me, and she still doesn't talk to me except to complain about something I've done. The only positive change in her manner I've noticed is that the aggravating cult smile seems to have permanently disappeared from her face.

I never recovered my wonderful raincoat. When I asked my parents to replace it, it was explained to me that I could not expect to be bought frivolous extras when poor, destitute Myra needed all the basics in life. My mother even threw what she called a Coming-Home Shower—a family party in Myra's honor. All the aunts and girl cousins and grandmothers and women friends showed up with gifts for Myra—"to replace what those evil culties had stolen from the poor child."

Disgust does not begin to describe what I felt about the treatment Myra was getting. Irene skipped the Myra celebration and took me out to lunch. She showed me a minor but effective martial-arts trick called the Tibetan Ear Kvetch. I don't know if I'll ever use it on Myra, but learning it made me feel better about everything.

Irene and Clara have become very good friends. Since Clara didn't drop dead from exhaustion during the escape, Irene decided she was in terrific physical condition. Clara attributes her excellent health to all the years sleeping outdoors and walking miles, carting around those heavy shopping bags.

Irene invited Clara, Samson the parakeet and the shopping bags to stay in Irene's apartment while the two women began a work-out program. For a number of months, Irene and Clara jogged all over town in the morning and spent every afternoon at the health club. For Christmas, Irene gave Clara a set of matched canvas shopping bags with zipper compartments. They left for the Far East as soon as Clara got her brown belt in karate. I think they went to Tibet. They wouldn't say. All Irene would tell me was that she was going to solve a case which involved steep mountains and bandits. I wish I could have gone with them.

Pete, alias Sonny Perfect II, left the Garden of Perfection that night with a pocket full of computer disks containing Daddy Perfect's financial records. He sold the story of his life as a cult kid to a national magazine and turned the records over to the federal government. That proved to be his most lucrative deal, because the Internal Revenue Service will pay any citizen who reports a tax evader a percentage of the back taxes collected. Daddy Perfect owed the government a bundle. Pete negotiated well and received 50 percent.

Pete says he doesn't feel bad about finking on his family because they got their money by taking advantage of people. He even took a newspaper ad out, offering to return love gifts to people who were bilked by the Perfects, but no one came forward. Pete thinks they were too embarrassed to admit being cheated.

It turns out Pete really liked Jane very much. After the

government sold off the cult's cars, houses, property and stores and emptied the Perfects' bank accounts, took its cut and handed Pete a check for an enormous amount of money, Pete gave Jane half.

Living in the Garden of Perfection most of his life, Pete never had any formal education. Nevertheless, he got accepted at several colleges because of his experiences and the book he wrote. As George says, Pete is one smart dude. Both Jane and Pete are now enrolled in the same expensive college. They live in an off-campus building in beautiful apartments.

The dogs have also done very well since their cult days. Prince lives with Pete. King and Godzilla have been adopted by the Vogels, who have installed a swinging dog door so the two former killers can have the run of the estate. The dogs have gotten fairly fat and very lazy. They keep George company when the Vogels travel, and they protect the place when they are not sleeping.

As far as I know, the parakeet Samson is traveling through the Far East with Clara and Irene in a specially built, insulated, padded and heated cage/shopping bag. I assume he is happy.

That leaves Lucrezia Borgia. My parents were so distracted by Myra's return that Lucrezia Borgia had been living in our house for two weeks before they noticed she was around. By that time, it was impossible for them to come up with the usual parental objection to pets—the one that goes, "She'll be too much trouble." How can a pet you don't even notice be trouble?

The expense of feeding her and taking her to the veterinarian has been covered by my fee. Pete insisted on paying me a sizable chunk of money, even though he had not been my official client. I am not independently wealthy, but the interest from my new savings account buys a whole lot of dog kibble.

Sometimes I think I should change Lucrezia Borgia's name

to something nicer—like Pumpkin, in honor of the vegetable which gave its life so that we might be free. But I kind of like the sound of Lucrezia Borgia. It's a good, tough name for a detective's dog.

With the Temple of Perfection shut down and the members drifting away and the bad publicity and the story of Sonny II's life and the loss of their fortune to the federal government, you would think that Mommy and Daddy Perfect would fade into the sunset. Wrong. Wrong. Wrong.

Mommy Perfect published her diaries. The book was entitled *Evil Is as Evil Does: The Diary of a Perfect Swine.* Daddy Perfect published his life story. It was called *Daddy Perfect and the Devil.* The books were essentially the same. They told —in great detail—about how each had been an evil person and how each had found God and reformed. Both books were published at the same time the government prosecuted both Perfects for tax evasion. There was a whole lot of publicity about the cult and the tax case. Daddy and Mommy Perfect appeared on radio talk shows all over the country. Soon you could tune them in during the day on television talk shows. In a few months, they could be seen chatting away on the late-night television talk shows. Naturally their books got onto *The New York Times* best-seller list. That's when Daddy and Mommy Perfect made the cover of *People* magazine.

The day that happened, I turned on the television and saw Daddy Perfect, dressed in electric blue, magical beams of brightness emanating from his beard, talking to a reporter on the five o'clock news. Mommy Perfect stood smiling at his side. Daddy Perfect was explaining to the reporter how he intended to build a temple to the Lord in the form of a Holy Television Station—now that he was a reformed man. He was about to embark on a project to battle the devil and would need the love gifts of all those devil-fighting, good-hearted folks in television land.

The TV reporter cut Daddy Perfect off just as he was about to give a mailing address where one could send money.

I was disgusted. Irene hadn't left yet for the Far East, so I grabbed my bicycle and rode over to her house. Irene's living room was filled with suitcases, climbing gear and overflowing canvas shopping bags.

"So?" she said, after I explained what I had just seen. "Why is it bothering you?"

"What we did was useless. We risked our lives for nothing. He's still at it, and now he's on national television. In fact, we probably helped him get there because of what we did."

"You did, Niece. It was your case."

I got more depressed. "I did. You're right. It's my fault."

"There is no fault."

"Yes there is. Daddy Perfect is going to lure people in all over again—just like an enormous, poisonous spider."

"So?" Irene was being infuriating.

"So that's terrible! Why wasn't he stopped? Nothing affected him. All he lost was some money, which he is making back again—and more!"

Irene took me into the kitchen and poured some tepid tsampa into a bowl for me. I played with my spoon while we talked.

"The point is, Niece, that you did a whole lot of good. You got your silly sister out of there, and you also managed to free Clara, Jane, Pete and the four dogs. You gained a loyal and intelligent dog friend and observed a number of important and interesting Tibetan mind skills in operation.

"You have provided ME with a fine companion—Clara. I will always be grateful for that. You gave George a chance to participate in a splendid adventure, and you made it possible for him to have constant company and protection in that beautiful but lonely house.

"You want a neat ending, Niece. There are no neat endings."

"What about justice? What about fairness? What about all those new suckers the Perfects are working on?"

"Remember the pumpkin and the car—the cosmic joke? This is part two."

"But I feel as if it's on me!"

"That's how it is with cosmic jokes."

"I don't think I like cosmic jokes, Irene."

"Neither did your great-great-grandfather—they're too illogical and unpredictable—flitting here and there, landing wherever the spirit dictates. I think I am the only Holmes in recent history who truly appreciates cosmic jokes."

"What do you think Great-great-grandfather Sherlock would think of my first case, Irene?"

"He'd think you did a smashing job. In fact, he'd be the one giving you this farewell gift. Open it at home, little Holmes. Sentiment makes me nervous. I'll send you a postcard." Then Irene did something very out of character. She hugged me.

I rode home as fast as I could, balancing the big box on the handlebars. On my bed, I tore off the wrapping. I lifted the lid, and there it was—my black detective raincoat. No, it was a better black detective raincoat. It had more buttons and more pockets and much more class. It was made of the softest, shiniest leather in the world.

I put it on, turned the collar up and went outside. Lucrezia Borgia and I took a long, slow walk around the neighborhood to celebrate the completion of our first successful case.